FOREWORD

Sherlock Holmes and Dr. Watson are characters created by Sir Arthur Conan Doyle and are now in the public domain. This collection offers new adventures and investigations imagined by the author.

This book brings together several entirely fictional stories. While they are inspired, in part, by facts that may come from reality, all these stories are fictionalized and feature fictional characters, places, and events borrowed from the work of Sir Arthur Conan Doyle and his series of short stories and novels featuring Sherlock Holmes.

Any resemblance to real persons or events is entirely coincidental.

CW01499168

TABLE OF CONTENTS

Sherlock Holmes

Of Shadows and Wonders

Aurélien Louvet

THE CHRONOFABULIST

I

It was during one of those November evenings when London seems to wrap itself in a grayish shroud. The rain, fine and persistent, drummed against the windows of 221B Baker Street, while the wind whistled through the smallest cracks of our lodgings. A generous fire crackled in the fireplace, casting dancing shadows on the papered walls of our sitting room.

Sherlock Holmes sat in his favorite armchair, legs stretched toward the hearth, leafing through the evening papers with ostentatious indifference. Since the conclusion of our previous case three weeks earlier, my friend had fallen into that particular state I knew all too well. His mind, comparable to a high-precision engine, was idling, consuming its own energy for lack of a problem worthy of his faculties.

"Look at this, Watson," he said suddenly, waving the newspaper. "A jewelry theft in Mayfair, a disappearance in Whitechapel, and this so-called espionage affair at the Austrian Embassy. Scotland Yard bustles about like an overturned anthill, and yet..."

"Yet nothing deserves your attention?" I ventured, looking up from my medical treatise.

"Exactly. Crimes of distressing banality." He tossed the newspaper onto the table with an impatient gesture. "The jewelry thief is obviously the new valet-note the absence of any mention of forced entry. The Whitechapel disappearance concerns a young girl who has simply fled from a tyrannical father-observe the paltry reward offered for her return. As for the espionage affair, it is merely a stratagem by the second secretary to conceal his own negligence."

I couldn't help smiling. Even in his idleness, Holmes couldn't resist exercising his gifts of observation and deduction.

"I fear, my dear friend," I said, "that you are condemned to a few additional days of forced rest. Which, by the way, would be beneficial after the exhaustion of our last adventure."

Holmes was about to reply when Mrs. Hudson knocked at the door and entered with a tray in hand.

"A messenger has just delivered this letter for you, Mr. Holmes," she announced. "He insisted on its urgent nature."

Holmes quickly seized the envelope. In the lamplight, I saw his eyebrows rise slightly-a tiny but revealing sign of his sudden interest.

"Thank you, Mrs. Hudson." He examined the envelope from all angles before opening it with the blade of his ivory letter knife. "Let's see what we have here..."

The envelope was made of high-quality vellum paper, bearing the seal of Cambridge University. Holmes extracted two sheets covered with cramped, nervous handwriting. As he read, I saw his face animate with a gleam I knew well-that of awakened intellectual interest.

"Watson," he said at last after reading the letter twice, "what do you think of time travel?"

The question caught me off guard. "Time travel? You mean like in Mr. Wells's recent work?"

"Precisely. This letter is from Dr. Alaric Vorne, a physicist at Cambridge and respected member of the Royal Society. He presents me with a most singular case." Holmes handed me the letter. "Read it yourself."

I took the sheets and began to read:

"Dear Mr. Holmes,

Although we have never met, your reputation as a logician and investigator of mysteries that defy common understanding prompts me to seek your assistance in a matter which, I am convinced, deserves your attention.

For six months, scientific circles and certain London salons have been agitated by the appearance of an individual calling himself Gideon Blacksmith. This man claims to have been born in 1789 and to have left his era-specifically the year 1824-thanks to a device of his invention which he calls an 'ethereal chronometer.'

If I write to you today, it is not simply to denounce what might be just another charlatan in our London so fertile in frauds. The situation is far more serious. Blacksmith has succeeded in convincing several minds I thought rational. Educated, wealthy, and generally skeptical persons have fallen under his sway.

He organizes private sessions where he presents what he claims to be irrefutable proof of his temporal journey: a diary authenticated by experts, inexplicable photographs, and above all, historical knowledge so precise and obscure that it defies conventional explanation.

More troubling still, he occasionally predicts events which, invariably, occur as announced.

I have alerted Scotland Yard, but they refuse to intervene, considering this merely a case of charlatanism that does not fall within their jurisdiction as long as no obvious crime is observed. Yet Blacksmith has already founded what he calls 'The Brotherhood of Ethereal Travelers,' whose members pay considerable sums to be 'prepared for the journey.'

I fear we are witnessing the emergence of a dangerous cult, exploiting the credulity and despair of vulnerable people, particularly wealthy widows and widowers to whom Blacksmith implicitly promises reunions with their departed loved ones.

If you consent to examine this case, I can procure an invitation to his next private session, scheduled for Thursday next.

In hope of a favorable response,

Dr. Alaric Vorne, Ph.D.

Professor of Theoretical Physics

Cambridge University"

I set down the letter, perplexed. "This is indeed a strange case, Holmes. Do you think it's actually an elaborate form of charlatanism?"

Holmes had joined his fingertips under his chin, in that meditative posture I knew so well. "The question is not whether time travel is possible, Watson, but how a man can convince rational minds that he has accomplished it."

"So you intend to accept this investigation?"

"How could I resist?" A fleeting smile illuminated his austere face. "A supposed time traveler who manages to mystify Cambridge scientists! That promises to be stimulating." He rose with a bound, suddenly revitalized. "Note several interesting elements in this letter, Watson. First, the paper-first-quality vellum, but the fibers reveal the tremors of a hand accustomed to precise writing. Our Dr. Vorne was manifestly agitated while composing this missive."

Holmes approached the window, contemplating the rain streaming down the glass. "Next, notice that he mentions 'inexplicable photographs.' How could a man supposedly born in 1789 appear in daguerreotypes predating the very invention of this process? And these predictions that come true... that suggests either a network of accomplices or a manipulation of events."

Turning briskly toward me, he added: "But what intrigues me most of all is this ability to convince educated persons. Fools are legion, Watson, but to seduce the intellect of men of science requires an uncommon talent."

I nodded, already captivated by this new enigma. "What do you plan to do?"

"First, reply to Dr. Vorne to accept his invitation." Holmes settled at his desk and took up his pen. "Then, before Thursday, we must familiarize ourselves with this Gideon Blacksmith. I suggest a visit to the Diogenes Club tomorrow-my brother Mycroft may have heard of this individual."

Holmes paused, his pen suspended above the paper. "One last thing, Watson. If you have no engagements for Thursday evening, I would welcome your company. Charlatans are sometimes dangerous when they feel threatened."

"I wouldn't miss this adventure for anything," I replied enthusiastically.

Holmes smiled again, then bent over his paper. The rain continued to beat against the windows, but the atmosphere of our sitting room had transformed. The languor had been succeeded by that electric tension that always preceded our most fascinating investigations. The case of the "Chronofabulist," as I decided to name it in my journal, had just begun.

The next morning, the weather had somewhat improved. A pale autumn sun was attempting to pierce through the clouds that still hung over London. As agreed, Holmes and I left Baker Street to visit the Diogenes Club, that singular refuge where Mycroft Holmes was a regular.

"My brother, Watson, occupies a unique position in the administration," Holmes reminded me as our hansom progressed through the still-damp streets. "His knowledge of any unusual social phenomenon in London is often more complete than that of Scotland Yard."

The Diogenes Club remained one of the strangest places in London. In this sanctuary of silence, where speaking outside the "Strangers' Room" constituted grounds for immediate expulsion, gathered the most misanthropic and distinguished men of the capital.

Mycroft Holmes awaited us in said room, his massive silhouette nearly filling an armchair that seemed too narrow for him. His eyes, as piercing as his brother's but half-closed by indolence, animated at our entrance.

"Ah, Sherlock. And Dr. Watson. I suspected this Blacksmith affair would eventually interest you," he declared without preamble, once again confirming the extraordinary anticipatory faculties of the Holmes brothers.

"So you know this individual?" Sherlock asked, taking a seat.

"Not personally. But his name has crossed certain governmental circles." Mycroft joined his pudgy fingers over his waistcoat. "It seems this Blacksmith has among his followers Lady Carrington, whose late husband was an advisor to the Colonial Office. This has raised concerns about possible indiscretions."

"Has anyone investigated his background?" Holmes asked.

"Superficially. Gideon Blacksmith seems to have appeared from nowhere about eight months ago. No records, no official trace before that date. He first gained notice in literary salons, then scientific ones, where his erudition impressed."

"And his temporal claims?"

Mycroft gave an ironic smile. "Initially, he presented himself simply as a specialized historian. Only after establishing his credibility did he gradually introduce the idea of his... journey." He paused. "But I doubt it's merely his story that interests you, Sherlock."

"Indeed. Tell me about his victims-or should I say, his followers."

"A disparate group but with common characteristics: substantial personal fortune, recent emotional trauma for most, and a fascination with modern scientific advances. Lady Carrington, Lord Pembrooke, Sir William Ashton-recently widowed, Judge Harrington's widow..."

"Lady Harrington," interrupted Holmes. "Tell me about her."

"A brilliant woman, formerly an amateur mathematician before her marriage. Her husband died eighteen months ago. Considerable fortune. She hosts receptions where Blacksmith is regularly invited." Mycroft removed a small notebook from his pocket. "She happens to be giving a tea this afternoon at her residence in Belgrave Square."

Holmes rose promptly. "That's providential. Watson, it seems we have a social invitation to honor."

Mycroft closed his notebook. "One last thing, Sherlock. Last week, Blacksmith predicted with disturbing accuracy the collapse of a scaffolding on Oxford Street-three days before the incident. No casualties, fortunately, but it considerably strengthened his credibility."

"Interesting," murmured Holmes. "Very interesting."

Lady Harrington's home in Belgrave Square embodied the discreet elegance of English aristocracy. An austere butler showed us into a drawing room where half a dozen people were already gathered around a woman in her fifties, whose fine face retained traces of classical beauty and intelligence.

Holmes had introduced himself as Mr. Sherrinford, an antiquarian, and had presented me as his physician friend. Our hostess welcomed us with measured politeness.

"Mr. Sherrinford, Dr. Watson, welcome. Professor Lewis informed me of your interest in our modest discussions."

"Professor Lewis" was in fact a former client of Holmes who had provided us with this improvised introduction.

"Your reputation as a patron of the sciences precedes you, Lady Harrington," Holmes replied with a cordiality that always surprised me when he adopted a persona.

"You flatter me. I merely bring together curious minds." She guided us toward the circle of her guests. "We were just discussing the implications of Lord Kelvin's ethereal theory on our understanding of time."

The conversation that followed quickly went beyond me, drifting toward scientific considerations where Holmes, to my great surprise, showed himself perfectly at ease. I discreetly observed the other guests: two university professors judging by their bearing, a clergyman, and a middle-aged couple whose elegance betrayed considerable fortune.

Only after half an hour of discussion did Holmes subtly steer the conversation toward the subject that interested us.

"I recently heard of a certain Mr. Blacksmith who apparently has fascinating theories about the nature of time," he said with studied nonchalance.

A sudden silence fell over the assembly. The guests exchanged glances I could not interpret with certainty.

"You know Mr. Blacksmith?" Lady Harrington finally asked, her gaze suddenly sharper.

"Only by hearsay," Holmes replied. "His ideas seem... controversial."

"As are all great ideas at their beginnings, Mr. Sherrinford." Lady Harrington's voice had taken on an almost defensive tone. "Galileo too was mocked in his time."

"So you've met him personally?"

"I've had that privilege. Mr. Blacksmith is a remarkable man."

"A charlatan, that's what he is," the clergyman suddenly intervened vehemently. "Forgive me, Lady Harrington, but I cannot remain silent in the face of this imposture. Claiming to have traveled through time is a heresy compounded by fraud!"

"Reverend Chambers hasn't yet had the opportunity to attend a complete demonstration," our hostess explained calmly. "He might judge differently if he had seen what we have seen."

"And what exactly have you seen?" asked Holmes.

Lady Harrington hesitated, then her gaze lit up with a fervor that made me uncomfortable. "Evidence, Mr. Sherrinford. Irrefutable evidence that a man has crossed the barrier of time. I have held in my hands his diary, written in 1824, describing events that no historian had remembered-and which I personally verified in private archives."

"Fascination with history, that's all," grumbled the reverend.

"And how do you explain that he described to me with absolute precision the sapphire brooch my late husband had given me during our honeymoon? A unique piece, never photographed, lost in a burglary fifteen years ago?"

This revelation seemed to momentarily silence the reverend. The wealthy couple exchanged a knowing look.

"You seem convinced of the authenticity of his claims," observed Holmes.

"I was skeptical, Mr. Sherrinford. Terribly skeptical. As you would be in my place. But after attending his private demonstrations..." She paused, then added in a lower voice: "Mr. Blacksmith is giving a session next Thursday. If you're sincerely interested, I might be able to get you invited."

"It would be an honor," Holmes replied with measured enthusiasm.

As we took our leave an hour later, armed with the precious invitation, I couldn't help noticing the change in Holmes's attitude. His face had regained that concentrated expression I knew so well.

"What do you think?" I asked once in the hansom taking us back to Baker Street.

"I think, Watson, that we're dealing with a remarkably intelligent man. This brooch story is particularly interesting."

"Do you believe he might really know things he shouldn't know?"

Holmes smiled slightly. "There are many ways to obtain private information, my dear friend. Servants talk, diaries can be consulted, old family albums examined. What intrigues me more is Lady Harrington's absolute conviction. This woman is no fool-Mycroft mentioned her talents in mathematics. To convince her, our man must have elaborated a particularly sophisticated system of proofs."

"So you think it's a fraud?"

"I don't yet have a definitive opinion. But I noticed Lady Harrington was wearing a ring with very particular symbolism-a serpent biting its own tail."

"An ouroboros," I murmured, recognizing this ancient symbol.

"Precisely. A symbol of eternity and perpetual cycles. And I observed the same ring on another guest's finger. I suspect it's the recognition sign of this 'Brotherhood of Ethereal Travelers' mentioned by Dr. Vorne."

Holmes looked out the hansom window, his eyes fixed on the busy streets of London. "Our Gideon Blacksmith isn't content with impressing his audience, Watson. He's creating disciples. And that, my friend, is infinitely more dangerous than a simple swindle."

The hansom stopped before our lodgings. As we descended, Holmes added: "Prepare yourself for Thursday, Watson. We're going to meet a man who claims to have traversed the centuries. And I intend to discover how he has managed to convince rational minds of such an impossibility."

II

Thursday arrived, bringing with it a fog so thick it seemed to have erased the very outlines of London. From our window, Baker Street appeared only as a succession of yellowish halos from the streetlamps, whose light struggled to pierce this opaque mist.

"Perfect weather for a session of mystification," commented Holmes, adjusting his tie. For the occasion, he had donned a suit of unusual elegance, completed by a tie pin adorned with a small emerald. "Our Blacksmith will surely appreciate this atmosphere conducive to apparitions."

"You seem in excellent spirits," I remarked while checking that my revolver was properly in place in my pocket. Experience had taught me that Holmes's investigations, even those that seemed most harmless, could take dangerous turns.

"How could I not be, Watson? Tonight, we will witness either the most extraordinary revelation in human history or a deception of remarkable ingenuity. In either case, the spectacle promises to be fascinating."

Our hansom deposited us before an imposing mansion in Mayfair, whose Georgian façade rose, ghostlike, in the mist. Lights shone in all the windows, creating a striking contrast with the surrounding darkness. A liveried servant welcomed us and collected our invitations before leading us through a richly decorated entrance hall.

"Sir William Ashton's residence," murmured Holmes. "Widowed for eighteen months, considerable fortune in the textile industry, and apparently a new patron of our time traveler."

We were shown into a vast salon where about twenty people had already gathered. I immediately recognized Lady Harrington, who was conversing in hushed tones with a slender, gray-haired man. Other guests, all dressed with an elegance that testified to their high social status, formed small groups whose conversations briefly interrupted at our entrance.

A closer observation revealed to me the presence of at least three ouroboros rings among the guests. Holmes, faithful to his character of Mr. Sherrinford, adopted an attitude of polite curiosity as we were introduced to our host.

Sir William Ashton was a robust man in his sixties, his face marked by what I judged to be a mixture of grief and feverish hope. He shook our hands with surprising vigor.

"Lady Harrington told me of your interest, Mr. Sherrinford. You arrive at just the right moment-we are witnessing a revolution in our understanding of the universe."

"I approach these questions with an open but rigorous mind," Holmes replied with a measured smile.

"As we all did at the beginning," agreed Sir William. "Skepticism is natural when faced with the extraordinary. But you'll see..."

He broke off as a sudden silence fell over the assembly. A servant had opened the double doors leading to an adjacent room, and all eyes turned in that direction.

"Ladies and gentlemen," announced Sir William, "please proceed to the library. Our esteemed guest is ready to begin."

Sir William Ashton's library was an impressive room, its walls entirely covered with leather-bound volumes. A space had been arranged in the center, where chairs placed in a semi-circle faced a small platform. On a table covered with black velvet were several objects I couldn't clearly distinguish from my position. The lighting, provided by dimmed gas lamps and a few strategically placed candles, created an atmosphere halfway between scientific salon and séance.

Holmes and I took seats in the second row. I noted that my friend had chosen a position offering an unobstructed view not only of the platform but also of all the spectators.

"Observe the reactions more than the spectacle itself," he whispered to me. "The regulars may betray what they anticipate."

Hardly had he spoken these words when a side door opened, and a man entered with measured steps.

Gideon Blacksmith perfectly matched the image I had formed of a gentleman from the early century. Tall and thin, he wore an impeccably tailored black suit in a style slightly outdated but elegant. His face, adorned with a short, carefully maintained beard, presented regular features dominated by intense blue eyes. His black hair, graying at the temples, was combed with meticulous precision. He might have been between forty and fifty, but his bearing and presence gave him a remarkable stature.

"My dear friends," he began in a deep, melodious voice with a slight accent I couldn't identify, "I thank you for your presence tonight."

He swept the audience with his gaze, pausing imperceptibly on Holmes before continuing:

"I see among us some new faces. Welcome to this quest for truth. I am not unaware of the skepticism my claims may provoke. In your place, I would have the same doubts."

Blacksmith took a few steps on the platform, his movements imbued with deliberate grace.

"I am not here to convince you with empty words. Words are ephemeral, theories abound, but only tangible evidence deserves your consideration."

He approached the table and lifted a veil that partially covered the objects.

"What I am about to present tonight is but a fraction of the evidence I have brought back from my journey. Not to dazzle you, but to invite you to consider the inconceivable: that the limits of time, as we perceive them, may be merely the bars of a cage that science can open."

Holmes leaned slightly forward, his intense gaze fixed on Blacksmith's hands. I noted that his fingers, fine and well-groomed, wore several antique rings, though none representing an ouroboros.

"Before anything else," Blacksmith resumed, "allow me to briefly explain my theory. Time is not a river flowing uniformly, but rather an ocean with multiple currents. At certain precise points, which I have baptized 'ethereal nodes,' these currents come close enough to allow, with considerable energy input, a passage from one era to another."

He then indicated a device placed on the table. It was a strange object, combining elements of clockwork and unknown electrical components. A central dial surrounded by several concentric rings was surmounted by a crystal sphere in which small bluish sparks danced.

"This is the ethereal chronometer. Its design required twenty years of work, between 1804 and 1824. The principles on which it operates would surpass the understanding of even the most brilliant physicists of your era, as they rely on discoveries that, for you, still belong to the future."

At these words, I heard a slight stifled chuckle from the back of the room. Turning discreetly, I noticed a bespectacled man shaking his head in disbelief. Blacksmith appeared to notice him as well.

"Skepticism is the cornerstone of science, sir," he said, addressing the man directly. "I do not ask you to take me at my word. Rather, observe this."

He manipulated some buttons on the device. The crystal sphere illuminated with a more intense glow, and a deep hum filled the room. The air around the chronometer seemed to distort slightly, like above a road in the heat of summer.

"What you observe is only an infinitesimal echo of the phenomenon that allowed me to traverse seventy-one years to arrive in 1895. A complete demonstration would require power I cannot generate under these conditions and would very certainly cause the collapse of this house."

The device emitted a sharp whistle, then gradually quieted. I had to admit the effect was impressive, but nothing indicated it was anything other than an ingenious electrical device.

Holmes observed the scene with remarkable intensity, his gaze alternating between the apparatus and Blacksmith's hands.

"Let us now turn to more substantial evidence," the latter continued.

He removed from a leather case a bound book whose worn cover testified to considerable age. "My personal journal, begun in 1812 and continued until the day of my... departure. In these pages I have recorded not only my research but also observations on daily life and the events of my era."

He carefully opened the volume to a marked page and handed it to Lady Harrington, seated in the front row.

"Madam, would you kindly read aloud the entry for April 13, 1821?"

Lady Harrington took the journal with reverence and began to read:

"'April 13, 1821. Witnessed a distressing spectacle this morning on Threadneedle Street. A crowd gathered before Marshton & Sons bank, whose failure was announced yesterday. Mr. Hatton, a merchant whom I know by sight, collapsed upon learning of the loss of his entire fortune. Dr. Fleming, present by chance, immediately bled him, but I fear the shock was fatal. Lady P., passing in her carriage, stopped to offer her smelling salts, a charitable gesture which elicited a few murmurs of approval..."'

She paused and handed the journal back to Blacksmith.

"This historical detail," he explained, "appears in no published work. The failure of Marshton is mentioned in financial archives, but the incident concerning Mr. Hatton remained unknown to historians. Yet I was able to confirm his death on that precise date through the parish registers of St. Mary Woolnoth, which can be consulted in the municipal archives."

He turned to the skeptical man. "Sir, if you doubt the authenticity of this document, I invite you to examine it. The paper, the ink, the cross-references with verifiable events-everything attests to its origin."

The man approached reluctantly and took the journal. After a careful examination, he returned it without comment, but his expression betrayed a certain unease.

Blacksmith continued his demonstration by extracting several documents from a portfolio: old letters, yellowed newspaper clippings, and finally, a daguerreotype which he presented with particular solemnity.

"This may be the most troubling evidence of my account. A photograph taken in 1843-after my departure, certainly, but by a process I had studied before my journey."

He circulated the daguerreotype among the audience. When it reached my hands, I saw that it showed a group of men in period clothing, posing in front of what appeared to be a laboratory. In the center of the group, a man unmistakably resembled Blacksmith, though younger by about ten years.

"How do you explain this?" asked an elderly lady. "You claim to have left your era in 1824, yet you appear in a photograph from 1843?"

"An excellent question, madam," Blacksmith replied with a smile. "Temporal travel is not as simple as your novelists describe it. There are... echoes, reverberations. A part of my essence remained anchored in my original era, continuing a parallel existence for a few decades after my principal departure. This phenomenon, which I have named 'temporal resonance,' also explains why some of my contemporaries reported seeing me after 1824, when my primary consciousness had already reached your era."

This explanation provoked murmurs in the audience. I glanced at Holmes, whose face remained impassive, but I knew my friend well enough to recognize the gleam of intense interest that shone in his eyes.

"I have saved my most convincing demonstration for last," announced Blacksmith. "As some of you already know, I occasionally have the ability to perceive fragments of the near future-an unexpected side effect of my journey through the temporal ether."

An expectant silence settled in the library.

"Tomorrow, at precisely 3:47 PM, a fire will break out in the warehouse of the Continental Trading

Company, on Billingsgate. The flames will destroy mainly the east wing of the building but will be contained before spreading to adjacent structures. Fortunately, as the warehouse is closed on Friday afternoons, no lives will be lost."

He pronounced these words with clinical precision, as if reporting an event that had already occurred rather than a prediction.

"I have recorded this vision in writing." He handed a sealed envelope to Sir William Ashton. "I request that you keep this document until tomorrow evening, when we can verify the accuracy of my prediction."

A shiver ran through the audience. I saw several guests exchange impressed looks, while others, still skeptical, whispered among themselves.

"I do not ask you to believe blindly," concluded Blacksmith. "Question, verify, seek alternative explanations. Truth does not fear careful examination. Meanwhile, I am at your disposal to answer your questions."

For nearly an hour, Blacksmith answered the guests' questions with remarkable ease, citing obscure historical details, elaborating his theory of time travel with convincing scientific vocabulary, and evoking his life in the early nineteenth century with a precision that seemed to defy any preparation.

Holmes, who had remained silent until then, finally raised his hand.

"Mr. Blacksmith, I am fascinated by your account. Allow me a question: how do you explain your adaptation to our era? Language, manners, social conventions have evolved considerably in seventy years."

Blacksmith smiled slightly. "A perceptive question, Mr. Sherrinford. My adaptation was not immediate. I spent my first six months in relative isolation, studying your era, its customs, its literature. I am fortunate to possess a natural facility for languages and social codes. Moreover, don't forget that even in 1824, we had gentlemen and intellectual discussions. Forms change, but the foundation of civilization remains recognizable."

"And what surprised you most in our modern era?" insisted Holmes.

Blacksmith's gaze became more distant. "Your technical advances, of course-domesticated electricity, instantaneous communications. But even more, your relationship with time itself. You live at a pace my contemporaries would have judged frenzied. The perpetual ticking of your pocket watches seems to dictate every moment of your existence."

The answer seemed to satisfy Holmes, who inclined his head slightly in thanks. The session continued for a few more minutes, then Sir William announced its conclusion, inviting those present to refresh themselves in the adjacent salon.

As the guests dispersed, I noticed that several approached Blacksmith individually, exchanging a few words in low voices. Holmes observed these interactions with sustained attention.

"What do you think?" I asked him when we found ourselves somewhat apart.

"A remarkable performance, Watson. Our man knows his subject perfectly and masters the art of persuasion. Did you notice his way of answering questions? Never directly defensive, always broadening the frame to include the questioner in his reasoning."

"And his evidence? The journal, the photograph..."

"Patience, my friend. I need to verify certain details before pronouncing judgment. But I've noted several interesting elements..." He broke off as Blacksmith approached us.

"Mr. Sherrinford, Dr. Watson," he greeted us with a slight nod. "I hope my presentation seemed... enlightening."

"Quite fascinating," Holmes replied. "Your mastery of historical details is impressive."

"History becomes much more alive when one has lived it," replied Blacksmith with an enigmatic smile. Then, lowering his voice slightly: "I understand you're interested in antiquities, Mr. Sherrinford. Perhaps I could provide some unique perspectives on certain pieces in your collection."

"That would be a pleasure," Holmes responded. "May I contact you soon about this?"

"Sir William will provide you with my details. Now, if you'll excuse me..."

Blacksmith moved away to join Lady Harrington, who was waiting for him near the door.

"A remarkable man," I commented.

"Indeed, Watson." Holmes observed Blacksmith with an almost palpable intensity. "A remarkable man... and potentially dangerous. Come, we have much to do before tomorrow afternoon."

"You plan to attend this predicted fire?"

The look Holmes gave me was imbued with a determination I knew well. "Watson, I plan to do much more than that. I plan to discover how it will be produced."

III

No sooner had we left Sir William Ashton's residence than Holmes hailed a hansom with an energy that contrasted with the apparent tranquility he had maintained throughout the session.

"Direction Whitechapel," he ordered the driver. "We'll get off at the corner of Commercial Street."

"Whitechapel? At this hour?" I exclaimed as the vehicle set off into the misty night. "I thought the fire was predicted for tomorrow afternoon."

"Precisely, my dear Watson." Holmes drew his pocket watch and examined it in the flickering light of the hansom's lantern. "Which gives us exactly seventeen hours and twenty-two minutes to discover how

"Are you convinced, then, that this is all a hoax?" I asked.

Holmes tucked away his watch and fixed me with his sharp gaze, in which I thought I detected a glimmer of amusement. "Would you prefer that I entertain the hypothesis of a man born during the reign of George III who has traversed the decades by means of a device of his own invention?"

"When put that way, the idea does seem absurd," I admitted.

"The elimination of the impossible, Watson. Whatever remains, however improbable, must be the truth. Now, time travel contradicts all known laws of physics. Elaborate fraud, carefully constructed illusion, psychological manipulation-these are phenomena whose existence is amply documented."

The cab carried us through the streets of London, deserted at this late hour. The fog had slightly lifted, revealing a sky where a few scattered stars shone between the clouds.

"This Blacksmith is remarkably convincing," I observed. "His device, this 'ethereal chronometer,' seemed to produce effects difficult to explain."

"Electrical and luminous effects similar to those observed in certain modern magical performances. I noticed the presence of an almost invisible metal wire connecting the device to his left boot. A foot-operated control mechanism, no doubt."

"And the journal? The historical details it contains?"

"A fascinating question, indeed." Holmes sank back in his seat, fingers joined under his chin. "Our man is either a forger of exceptional skill or a scholar who has devoted years to studying obscure historical details. Perhaps both. I intend to verify some of his assertions tomorrow morning at the British Library."

"What about that photograph in which he appears?"

"Ah, the photograph!" Holmes smiled. "Did you notice the peculiar odor emanating from his hands?"

"An odor?" I tried to recall. "Now that you mention it, there was indeed something... A chemical scent, faint but distinctive."

"Rosin mixed with traces of silver and photographic fixer. Our Blacksmith regularly handles photographic development equipment."

The cab slowed and stopped at the requested intersection. Holmes promptly paid our fare and led me through a maze of dark alleys, navigating with the ease that his encyclopedic knowledge of London afforded him.

"Where exactly are we going?" I asked, keeping my hand on the grip of my revolver. Whitechapel, especially at night, was not a neighborhood to venture into without precaution.

"To the Continental Trading Company. I want to examine the premises before our 'prophecy' is fulfilled."

After a few minutes of walking, we stopped before a vast building of red brick. Massive warehouses flanked a central structure topped by a stopped clock. The entire complex was shrouded in darkness, except for a lantern glowing faintly near a side entrance, where a night watchman dozed on a chair.

Holmes observed the place attentively, lingering particularly on the east wing that Blacksmith had specifically mentioned in his prediction.

"Interesting," he murmured. "Very interesting."

"What do you observe?" I whispered.

"This building presents several notable characteristics. First, its relative isolation-the adjacent structures are sufficiently distant that the predicted fire could be contained without causing major collateral damage. Second, this east wing is visibly the oldest, probably the least well maintained too. Finally..." He paused, squinting. "Do you see that window on the second floor? The glass has been recently replaced-it reflects light differently."

Before I could respond, Holmes resolutely approached the night watchman, adjusting his gait to appear slightly intoxicated.

"G'evening, friend!" he called with feigned joviality, adopting the accent of London's working-class neighborhoods. "Tough night for standing guard, ain't it?"

The watchman, an elderly man with a graying beard, started and straightened in his chair. "Hey there! What do you want?"

"Just some information, my good man," replied Holmes, taking a coin from his pocket which he flashed in the lantern light. "Haven't been any strange folks prowling around here these past few days? I'm looking for my cousin, see, a tall skinny fellow who tends to meddle in business that don't concern him."

The man hesitated, visibly tempted by the coin. "There was a fellow asking questions yesterday," he finally said. "A gentleman with an accent, not from around here. Wanted to know how we organized the guard shifts, and which days the warehouse closed."

"That might be him," Holmes nodded. "He didn't have a beard, piercing blue eyes?"

"No, that one was rather stocky, with a reddish mustache. But there was another fellow waiting for him further away, he matches more what you're describing."

Holmes handed him the coin. "Thank you kindly, my good man. If you happen to see either of them again, could you pass word to Tom at the 'Smoking Dog' on Dorset Street? There's another coin like this one waiting for you."

We walked away, Holmes resuming his normal gait once out of the watchman's sight.

"That confirms my suspicions," he murmured. "Our Blacksmith, or more likely one of his accomplices, has reconnoitered the premises. They've carefully chosen this warehouse-closed Friday afternoons, minimal security, old structure but isolated from neighboring buildings."

"You think they will deliberately cause the fire, then?"

"I'm certain of it. The question is how. But to discover that, we must first verify other aspects of this case. Let's return to Baker Street; we have a busy day tomorrow."

The next morning, Holmes had already departed when I came down for breakfast. A hastily scribbled note informed me that he had gone to the British Library and asked me to meet him at noon at Fairson's, in the Strand.

I joined him at the restaurant at the appointed time, finding him seated before a roast beef which he contemplated distractedly, evidently absorbed in thought.

"Ah, Watson!" he exclaimed upon seeing me. "I've made some most interesting discoveries."

"Regarding Blacksmith's journal?" I asked, taking a seat.

"Among other things. I verified the anecdote concerning the Marshton bank failure and the death of Mr. Hatton. The records indeed confirm these events, and even the presence of a Dr. Fleming at the scene. A remarkably obscure historical detail."

"That would argue for the journal's authenticity, wouldn't it?"

Holmes smiled. "Not necessarily. It only proves that our man has access to very specialized historical sources." He leaned toward me, lowering his voice. "I consulted a specialist in ancient manuscripts at the library. Without revealing the object of my investigation, I described Blacksmith's journal in detail. His conclusion is that a skilled forger could produce a convincing period document, but there are chemical tests that can identify the real age of the paper and ink."

"If only we could subject this journal to such tests," I sighed.

"Patience, Watson. I discreetly collected a tiny fragment during yesterday's session." Holmes displayed a barely visible piece of paper that he had carefully placed in an envelope. "My friend Dr. Ainslie, a chemist at Imperial College, is examining it as we speak."

"You are diabolical, Holmes," I couldn't help but remark with admiration.

"Simply methodological precaution." He consulted his watch. "We still have three hours before the prophesied fire. After lunch, I suggest we pay a visit to Lady Harrington. I have some questions for her concerning her late husband and Blacksmith's revelations on the subject."

Lady Harrington received us in the same salon where we had met her previously. Although she seemed surprised by our impromptu visit, she welcomed us with impeccable courtesy.

"Mr. Sherrinford, Dr. Watson, what a pleasant surprise. I hope that last night's demonstration made a favorable impression?"

"Absolutely fascinating," replied Holmes, still in character. "So convincing, in fact, that I wished to explore certain aspects further. You mentioned that Mr. Blacksmith revealed details to you about a sapphire brooch, a gift from your late husband?"

Lady Harrington's face softened. "Indeed. A memento very dear to my heart. Henry gave it to me in Venice, during our honeymoon in 1868. It was unique, set with a Ceylon sapphire surrounded by small pearls arranged in a crescent moon."

"And you say this jewel was stolen?"

"Yes, during a burglary in 1880. I was inconsolable-not for its material value, but for what it represented."

"May I ask how exactly Mr. Blacksmith brought up this brooch?" Holmes had adopted a gentle, almost compassionate tone.

Lady Harrington hesitated for a moment. "It was during a private session, shortly after our first meeting. He described the brooch with absolute precision, even mentioning the small scratch on the setting, the result of a fall on the Rialto Bridge." Her eyes glistened with contained tears. "He told me that Henry had spoken to him about this jewel, that he regretted its loss because he knew how much it meant to me."

"Mr. Blacksmith claims to communicate with the deceased, then?" I asked, surprised that this aspect had not been mentioned during the public demonstration.

"No, not exactly," she replied quickly. "He explains that the past, present, and future coexist simultaneously in the temporal ether. He sometimes perceives... echoes, impressions. They are not communications properly speaking, rather fragments of consciousness that persist."

Holmes nodded with apparent sympathy. "A comforting notion. Your husband held an important position, didn't he?"

"Henry was a judge on the High Court. A respected man, a man of integrity."

"Did he keep documents at your home? Sensitive files, perhaps?"

Lady Harrington slightly furrowed her brow. "He did indeed have an office here where he sometimes worked on his cases. But why do you ask, Mr. Sherrinford?"

"Simple professional curiosity," replied Holmes with a reassuring smile. "As an antiquarian, I'm interested in objects and documents that travel through time. Forgive my indiscretion."

We took our leave shortly after, with Lady Harrington cordially inviting us to return for a more intimate session of the "Brotherhood of Ethereal Travelers."

"What have you learned?" I asked once in the hansom taking us to the Billingsgate docks.

"Several significant things, Watson. First, the existence of this private session where Blacksmith revealed knowledge of the lost brooch-a session not mentioned in Dr. Vorne's correspondence. Second, the fact that Lady Harrington's husband was a judge, with probable access to confidential information. Finally..." Holmes paused, peering through the window at the passing streets. "Did you notice the photograph on the mantelpiece?"

"The one of the elderly couple? Lady Harrington's parents, I assume."

"No, Watson. The one of the young man in uniform-her son, presumably. A Royal Navy officer, judging by the stripes. And in that photograph, distinctly visible, Lady Harrington was wearing the famous sapphire brooch."

I suddenly understood. "You think Blacksmith had access to this photograph?"

"It's a possibility. But let's not jump to hasty conclusions. We're approaching Billingsgate, and it's almost time for our rendezvous with our time traveler's prophecy."

The Continental Trading Company warehouse stood, massive and austere, in the fading light of the afternoon. As expected, the establishment seemed closed this Friday, with only a guard visible near the main entrance. Holmes had insisted that we position ourselves at a prudent distance, in an alley offering an unobstructed view of the east wing.

"It is three-forty," murmured Holmes, consulting his watch. "If Blacksmith's prediction is to be fulfilled, we shall soon see something."

We didn't have to wait long. At precisely three forty-five, a figure emerged furtively from a service door on the side of the building. The man-for it was certainly a man, of medium build and dressed in a long dark coat-cast a circular glance before moving away rapidly in the opposite direction from us.

"Wait here," ordered Holmes as he sprang in pursuit.

I was about to protest when a flash caught my attention toward the warehouse. An orange glow appeared in one of the windows on the second floor, at first faint, then increasingly intense. Within seconds, flames became visible, licking the window frames.

The guard raised the alarm, frantically ringing the fire bell that resonated in the damp air of the docks. Cries rose from the neighboring buildings, and soon men came running with buckets.

I remained at my post, torn between the desire to assist and Holmes's instructions. The fire spread rapidly through the east wing, exactly as Blacksmith had predicted. A thick black smoke now rose in the sky, visible for hundreds of yards around.

The first firefighters arrived about fifteen minutes after the start of the blaze. With remarkable efficiency, they deployed their equipment and began to fight the flames which, as our time traveler had announced, remained confined to the east wing of the building.

Holmes reappeared only an hour later, when the fire was almost under control. His face bore traces of the chase-a few scratches on his cheek and a misshapen hat testified to an altercation.

"Did you capture the man?" I asked eagerly.

"No," he admitted, out of breath. "He knew the area too well. After leading me through a maze of alleys, he jumped into a boat that was waiting for him on the Thames."

"Did you at least identify him?"

"I only caught a fleeting glimpse of his face, but it was enough. A stocky man with a reddish mustache-matching the description given by the night watchman. And look what I found, dropped from his pocket during our chase."

Holmes handed me a small metal object which I examined with curiosity. It was a miniature clockwork mechanism, connected to what appeared to be a chemical triggering system.

"A time-delay incendiary device," explained Holmes. "Ingenious and almost undetectable once the evidence is consumed by the flames. Our man probably installed it yesterday or this morning, set to trigger at the precise time mentioned by Blacksmith."

I contemplated the partially ruined warehouse, whose last flames were being smothered under jets of water. "So the fire was not an accident, nor a prophetic vision, but a deliberate criminal act?"

"Exactly, Watson. And now we have proof that our supposed time traveler is involved in a network that doesn't hesitate to commit acts of material destruction to lend credence to his alleged supernatural faculties." Holmes carefully pocketed the mechanism. "This little device will be our first tangible element against Blacksmith."

"What do we do now?"

"We return to Baker Street. I'm expecting Dr. Ainslie's response regarding the journal sample, and I've telegraphed my brother Mycroft for information on any possible background of our man. If my suspicions are correct, Gideon Blacksmith was no more born in 1789 than you or I."

Holmes's gaze had that particular intensity that presaged the imminent resolution of a puzzle. "Our time traveler is beginning to leave very tangible traces in the present, Watson. And unlike time, traces can be followed."

Back at Baker Street, we found two messages awaiting Holmes. The first, a note from Dr. Ainslie regarding the analysis of the paper fragment; the second, a telegram from Mycroft containing these simple words: "Information available. Diogenes. 8pm. M.H."

Holmes read Dr. Ainslie's note with sustained attention, a smile of satisfaction gradually forming on his austere face.

"As I suspected," he murmured, handing me the document. "Read for yourself, Watson."

The note was written in the precise style of a man of science:

"Dear Holmes,

Analysis of the submitted fragment reveals paper composed of wood fibers treated by an industrial process that postdates 1860. The chemical composition of the ink contains traces of aniline black, a synthetic pigment discovered in 1863.

These elements are incompatible with an authentic document from 1820-1824.

The apparent aging results from deliberate treatment: immersion in a tea solution, then exposure to smoke and application of a resinous substance containing pulverized amber.

This is unquestionably a forgery, albeit one executed with remarkable skill.

Sincerely,

Dr. H. Ainslie

Department of Analytical Chemistry

Imperial College"

"So that definitively confirms the journal is a fake," I remarked as I set down the note.

"A masterfully executed fake," Holmes specified. "The artificial aging process described by Ainslie is particularly sophisticated. Our man is not a simple charlatan, but a first-rate forger."

"That doesn't explain how he knows these obscure historical details."

"No, indeed." Holmes paced the sitting room, hands crossed behind his back. "It suggests considerable erudition or privileged access to unpublished sources. I have a few theories on the subject, but let's wait for Mycroft's information before speculating further."

He paused, contemplating the clockwork mechanism he had placed on the table. "This little masterpiece also deserves our attention. A time-delay incendiary device of exceptional precision. Look at the fineness of the gears, Watson. This is the work of a skilled watchmaker."

"Or a former watchmaker reconverted into a time traveler," I couldn't help adding with a touch of irony.

Holmes smiled. "Watchmaking would indeed be a useful skill for someone claiming to manipulate time." He examined the mechanism under his magnifying glass. "See this tiny mark on the main spring? The initials 'G.F.'-probably the manufacturer."

"Does that give us a lead?"

"Potentially. I know three watchmakers in London whose initials match: George Finchley, Gustav Faber, and Gabriel Fontaine. The latter, a Swiss established in Clerkenwell, is particularly renowned for his precision mechanisms."

Holmes consulted his watch. "We have a few hours before my appointment with Mycroft. I suggest we pay a visit to Mr. Fontaine."

Gabriel Fontaine's workshop occupied a modest shop in the watchmakers' district of Clerkenwell. Dozens of clocks and watches adorned the walls, their collective ticking creating a curious mechanical symphony. Behind a counter cluttered with tools, a man in his sixties, wearing magnifying glasses fixed on a headband, was working on a mechanism of breathtaking complexity.

"Mr. Fontaine?" Holmes called.

The watchmaker looked up, raising his glasses to his forehead. His weathered face lit up with a welcoming smile.

"Gentlemen, what can I do for you? A watch to repair, perhaps?"

Holmes took out the mechanism he had recovered and placed it gently on the counter. "I would like to know if you recognize this workmanship."

Fontaine picked up the piece and examined it with the practiced eye of a professional. His expression shifted from curiosity to recognition, then to a certain apprehension.

"Where did you find this?" he asked, suddenly wary.

"This object is connected to an ongoing investigation," Holmes replied with quiet authority. "Is it your work, Mr. Fontaine?"

The watchmaker hesitated, then nodded slowly. "The main gear, yes. I recognize my work. But I didn't assemble this... device."

"For whom did you make this gear?"

"A regular customer, Mr. Bolin. Geoffrey Bolin. He regularly orders precision parts, supposedly for scientific research." Fontaine set down the mechanism. "I never questioned the use he made of them."

"Could you describe this Mr. Bolin?" asked Holmes.

"A stocky man, in his forties, reddish mustache. Always well-dressed, knowledgeable about watchmaking. He often mentions that he works for a gentleman interested in 'advanced temporal mechanisms.'"

"And have you ever met this gentleman?"

"Only once. An elegant man, distinguished, with aristocratic manners. He came with Bolin about a year ago, examined my work, and placed a substantial order for specialized components."

"Could you recognize him?" Holmes took out a sketch he had made, depicting Blacksmith with striking resemblance.

Fontaine adjusted his glasses. "Yes, that's him. Although in this drawing, he seems younger than I remember."

"One last question, Mr. Fontaine. Do you know where this Mr. Bolin resides?"

"He never mentioned his personal address, but he sometimes picked up his orders at a workshop near Camden Town. An old printing house, I believe, on Parkway."

Leaving the shop, Holmes was visibly satisfied. "We're making progress, Watson. This Geoffrey Bolin is manifestly the man I pursued after the fire-Blacksmith's technical accomplice. And now we have an address to explore."

The former printing house in Camden Town turned out to be a dilapidated building whose ground floor windows were obscured by thick curtains. A worn sign indicated *"Bolin & Sons - Precision Work,"* but nothing suggested regular commercial activity.

After observing the place for nearly half an hour without detecting any sign of life, Holmes decided to adopt a more direct approach. He knocked vigorously on the door. No response came. He then examined the lock.

"A simple tumbler lock, Watson. Under other circumstances, I would suggest waiting for a warrant, but given the nature of the case and the probable involvement in criminal arson..."

With a dexterity that never ceased to amaze me, Holmes manipulated a few thin metal rods extracted from his inside pocket. In less than a minute, the lock yielded.

"Stay alert," he murmured as he gently pushed the door.

The interior was plunged into semi-darkness. A strong odor of chemicals and dust permeated the air. Holmes took out his dark lantern and directed its beam around us.

What we discovered exceeded my most extravagant expectations. The vast room had been transformed into a workshop combining metalwork, photography, and what appeared to be a chemistry laboratory. A long central table held precision instruments, flasks containing various liquids, and several devices whose function completely escaped me.

"Fascinating," murmured Holmes as he examined the objects one by one. "This is our forger's lair."

One corner of the room had been set up as a photographic darkroom, with developing trays, dryers where a few prints still hung, and a collection of photographic equipment of different models. On an adjacent workbench, glass plates bore markings in grease pencil.

"Look at this, Watson." Holmes held one of the dried photographs up to the light. "Do you recognize this image?"

It was a version of the photograph that Blacksmith had presented as evidence of his existence in 1843, but this one showed a notable difference: Blacksmith wasn't in it.

"It's the same scene, the same group, but without him," I observed, astonished.

"Exactly. The technique is known to specialized photographers-a carefully executed double exposure. First, they take an authentic old photograph, then reproduce it while superimposing the image of the subject to be inserted, in this case Blacksmith, photographed in a similar pose and identical lighting."

"A photographic trick," I murmured, impressed despite myself by the ingenuity of the process.

"A trick executed with exceptional mastery," Holmes specified. "Look at the quality of the fusion, the attention paid to the shadows. Our Bolin isn't just a watchmaker and an arsonist, he's also an artist of photography."

At the other end of the workshop, a desk was buried under documents. Holmes lingered there at length, leafing through registers and correspondence.

"The puzzle pieces are coming together, Watson. Here are receipts for the purchase of old paper from various antiquarians-ideal raw material for producing 'period' documents. And there, detailed notes on artificial aging techniques, consistent with Ainslie's observations."

He opened a drawer and took out a thick folder. "Ah! This is particularly revealing."

The folder contained several typewritten reports, each bearing a name I recognized as one of the members of Blacksmith's circle: Lady Harrington, Sir William Ashton, Lord Pembrooke...

"Private investigations," explained Holmes as he quickly skimmed through the documents. "Meticulous inquiries into the life, habits, and secrets of each potential target. Listen to this: 'Lady H. keeps a locket containing a lock of her late husband's hair. Invariably wears gloves in public since his death, exception made for musical evenings when she plays the piano-distinctive jewel then visible: sapphire brooch photographed in family albums consulted at her son's, Lt. Harrington.'"

"They spied on their victims!" I exclaimed indignantly.

"Meticulously. Collecting every personal detail, every secret, every object of sentimental value that could, once revealed by Blacksmith, appear to come from supernatural knowledge." Holmes closed the folder. "A methodical exploitation of vulnerability and grief."

He continued his exploration, opening a metal strongbox hidden under a tarpaulin. "And here is the motive for all this orchestration, Watson."

The strongbox contained several bundles of banknotes and an account book. Holmes examined it briefly.

"Substantial payments. *'Lady H. - 500 pounds - preparation for the journey.' 'Sir W.A. - 750 pounds - higher level of initiation.' 'Lord P. - 1200 pounds - contribution to the refinement of the chronometer.'* These are the membership fees for the Brotherhood of Ethereal Travelers. A large-scale swindle, methodically planned."

As we prepared to leave the premises, Holmes suddenly stopped, his attention drawn to a portrait hanging in a dark corner of the workshop. It was a framed photograph depicting two men in academic dress. One of them was undoubtedly a younger version of Blacksmith.

"Interesting," murmured Holmes, taking down the frame to examine the back. There was a half-erased inscription: *"Edmund and Garrett, Oxford, 1878."*

"Garrett? I thought his name was Gideon."

"Gideon Blacksmith is manifestly an assumed name, Watson. And this Edmund..." Holmes narrowed his eyes. "He seems familiar to me. Come, it's almost eight o'clock. My brother is waiting for us, and I suspect he may be able to complete this final piece of the puzzle."

Mycroft Holmes awaited us in the Strangers' Room at the Diogenes Club, his massive figure occupying his usual armchair. A thick folder of documents lay before him.

"Good evening, Sherlock. Doctor Watson." He greeted us with a slight nod. "I see from your expression that you've already made significant discoveries."

"Indeed, Mycroft. But I need your expertise to confirm certain hypotheses." Holmes handed him the photograph we had brought. "Do you recognize either of these men?"

Mycroft examined the picture without showing surprise. "Sir Edmund Blake, of course. Member of the Royal Society, occasional scientific advisor to the government. And his younger brother, Garrett Blake, who disappeared from academic circles after a scandal at Oxford. A matter of plagiarism, if my memory serves me correctly."

"Sir Edmund Blake," repeated Holmes. "A respectable man, then. Interesting. Do you have the information I asked for about our Gideon Blacksmith?"

Mycroft opened the folder and took out several documents. "Your intuition was correct, as usual. There is no Gideon Blacksmith in any official records before 1887, when the name first appears on the lease of a property in Bath."

"And before that?"

"Before that, we have a certain Garrett Blake, born in 1855 in Cambridge, younger son of Professor Harold Blake, a historian specializing in the Georgian period." Mycroft handed over an official document. "Brilliant student at Oxford until his expulsion in 1879. Then, nothing for nearly eight years, before his reappearance under the name of Blacksmith."

Holmes nodded, as if this revelation confirmed a hypothesis already formed. "And Sir Edmund? What is his current status?"

"Highly respected in scientific circles. Works primarily on electromagnetism, with some minor contributions to theoretical physics. Modest financial means for his rank-his family inheritance apparently having been squandered in unfortunate investments."

"Is he aware of his brother's activities?"

Mycroft shrugged. "Officially, no contact between them since the Oxford scandal. But my sources indicate a few discreet meetings over recent years."

"One last question, my dear brother. Have there been other incidents similar to today's fire? 'Prophesied' events that actually occurred?"

"Three documented cases," replied Mycroft, consulting his notes. "A scaffolding collapse on Oxford Street two weeks ago, as you already know. Before that, the flooding of a cellar at Cumberland Terrace, and a minor derailment of a freight train near Reading. No casualties, only property damage."

"Accidents orchestrated to lend credibility to Blacksmith's 'visions,'" concluded Holmes. "Ingenious and ruthless."

Mycroft closed his file. "What do you intend to do, Sherlock? This matter goes beyond simple fraud. If

Blake-or Blacksmith-continues to cause incidents to substantiate his claims, lives could be endangered."

"I have almost all the elements necessary to unmask him," replied Holmes. "I'm only missing one final piece: understanding how he obtained such precise historical knowledge, these details that even professional historians are unaware of."

"The answer may be simpler than you think," suggested Mycroft. "Remember who his father was."

"A historian specializing in the Georgian era," I murmured, suddenly understanding.

"Exactly, Dr. Watson," agreed Mycroft. "Professor Harold Blake was known for his collection of private archives, diaries, and correspondence from the 1800-1830 period. Documents never published, never catalogued, a mine of historical information inaccessible to the public."

"The perfect inheritance for a man seeking to pass himself off as a time traveler," concluded Holmes. "Thank you, Mycroft. Your help has been, as always, invaluable."

As we took our leave, Mycroft held his brother back by the arm. "Be careful, Sherlock. This man has much to lose if you unmask him. And his disciples are powerful."

"I know," replied Holmes. "That's why I intend to end this charade tomorrow."

Back at Baker Street, Holmes spent part of the evening writing notes and telegrams, while I recorded the day's events in my journal. Around midnight, he finally pushed away his papers and lit his pipe.

"Tomorrow, Watson, we shall witness the end of Mr. Gideon Blacksmith's career as a time traveler, alias Garrett Blake. I've learned that he's giving a private session for the members of his Brotherhood at Sir William Ashton's home. Our presence is already assured by Lady Harrington's invitation."

"What is your plan?" I asked, curious to know how he intended to unmask an impostor who had succeeded in convincing such educated people.

"A direct confrontation, supported by irrefutable evidence. I've telegraphed Lestrade to obtain his assistance-criminal arson falls under Scotland Yard's jurisdiction. Dr. Ainslie will also be present to testify about the falsification of the journal. As for the doctored photograph, the evidence we've recovered from Bolin's workshop will be sufficient to demonstrate the deception."

Holmes took a few puffs on his pipe, his gaze lost in the swirls of smoke. "The most difficult part will be breaking the psychological hold he exercises over his disciples. These people have invested not only their fortune but also their hopes and beliefs in this charlatan. Some may refuse to accept the truth, even when confronted with irrefutable evidence."

"And Sir Edmund Blake? What about his involvement?"

"A delicate question, indeed." Holmes frowned. "The evidence of his complicity is circumstantial, but his scientific status has certainly helped to indirectly legitimize his brother's claims. I suspect a tacit arrangement between them: Sir Edmund turns a blind eye to Garrett's activities, perhaps in exchange for a share of the profits that allows him to maintain his lifestyle."

He rose and went to the window, contemplating the deserted street below. "There's an almost Shakespearean dimension to this case, Watson. Two brothers-one respected but impoverished, the other talented but disgraced. One having chosen the path of academic legitimacy, the other that of lucrative imposture. And yet, their destinies remain intertwined."

I remembered then the motto that Holmes had often quoted to me: "The bonds of blood are the hardest to break."

"Get some rest, my friend," concluded Holmes, returning to his armchair. "Tomorrow awaits us with a day that promises to be memorable in the annals of scientific imposture."

As I went up to bed, I couldn't help thinking about the constellation of talents that Garrett Blake had deployed to construct his hoax: historical erudition, technical mastery, psychological manipulation, and that theatrical gift that had subjugated even cultivated minds. What a waste that such genius had gone astray in fraud, when he could have legitimately contributed to the advancement of knowledge!

But as Holmes had often reminded me, the most sophisticated crime is often merely the perverse diversion of aptitudes that, otherwise employed, could have nobly served humanity.

IV

The next morning, Holmes was already dressed and focused on his notes when I came down for breakfast. A pile of newspapers was spread on the table, with several articles circled in red pencil.

"Ah, Watson! Come see how our time traveler is making headlines."

I leaned over the newspapers he pointed out. The Billingsgate fire featured prominently in most of the dailies, but what particularly caught my attention was a small article in the Morning Chronicle:

"ASTONISHING PREDICTION FULFILLED... The fire that ravaged the east wing of the Continental Trading Company's warehouse yesterday was reportedly predicted with remarkable precision by a certain Mr. G.B., whose extraordinary faculties are the subject of animated discussions in certain London scientific circles. Several reliable witnesses affirm that the exact time and precise location of the disaster had been announced two days before the event. Does the phenomenon of premonition, long relegated to the domain of superstition, perhaps merit more rigorous examination by the scientific community?"

"The publicity machine is in motion," commented Holmes as he methodically buttered a piece of toast. "Note the careful yet suggestive wording, and the signature 'G.B.'-discreet enough to avoid accusations of charlatanism, but transparent enough for initiates to recognize Gideon Blacksmith."

"How can a respectable newspaper publish such insinuations?"

"The Chronicle has recently changed owners," replied Holmes. "Its new director, Lord Pembrooke, is among our Blacksmith's most convinced followers."

I shook my head, amazed at the extent of the alleged time traveler's influence.

"Our man is more dangerous than I initially thought," continued Holmes. "He's not content with extorting money from a few wealthy, gullible people. He's methodically building his public legitimacy, perhaps preparing for a larger-scale swindle."

"What exactly do we know about this Brotherhood of Ethereal Travelers?" I asked as I poured myself a cup of tea.

Holmes took a notebook from his pocket and consulted it. "According to my information, it currently has twenty-three regular members, all from the aristocracy or upper bourgeoisie. The annual membership fee is 100 pounds, plus 'special contributions' for access to higher levels of initiation. Some members have paid up to 2000 pounds to date."

"A considerable sum."

"Indeed. In total, I estimate that Blacksmith has already amassed between 15,000 and 20,000 pounds-a fortune that allows him to finance his elaborate stagings and buy various accomplices."

Holmes pushed aside his plate and checked his watch. "We have an appointment at ten o'clock with Lestrade at Scotland Yard. After that, I'd like us to visit

Sir Edmund Blake. His residence in Kensington is only a quarter of an hour away."

"Do you plan to confront him directly about his brother?"

"Not exactly. I first want to observe his reaction when we mention Blacksmith without revealing that we know of their family connection. The most revealing details often lie in what remains unsaid, Watson."

Inspector Lestrade welcomed us to his cramped office with his usual cordiality, tinged with that slight annoyance he invariably felt when Holmes interfered in Scotland Yard's affairs.

"The Billingsgate fire," he began after we had taken our seats. "My men have conducted the preliminary investigation. Officially, we're leaning toward an accident-probably an electrical problem or a carelessly discarded cigarette."

"And unofficially?" asked Holmes.

Lestrade shrugged. "Brigadier Jenkins, who directed the firefighters' intervention, confided to me that he noticed several distinct points of origin, which indeed suggests a deliberate act."

"Indeed." Holmes handed him the incendiary device we had recovered. "Here is the device used by the arsonist-a certain Geoffrey Bolin, accomplice to a man calling himself Gideon Blacksmith."

Lestrade examined the object with interest. "An ingenious mechanism. And you say this Blacksmith predicted the fire?"

"Precisely. It's an elaborate staging to convince wealthy dupes that he possesses paranormal faculties."

Holmes then summarized our investigation, explaining the journal fraud, the doctored photographs, and the orchestrated "predictions." Lestrade listened attentively, occasionally taking notes.

"A sophisticated swindle," he concluded. "But technically difficult to prosecute unless we can directly prove his participation in the criminal arson or extortion of money under false pretenses."

"That's why I need your cooperation tonight," replied Holmes. "Blacksmith is giving a private session at Sir William Ashton's, where he will undoubtedly present new 'evidence' of his extraordinary faculties. If we can catch him in the act of manipulation, with credible witnesses and material evidence..."

"I understand. You want me to be present, but discreetly."

"Exactly. With one or two plainclothes officers. I've also invited Dr. Ainslie for the chemical expertise on the journal, and I hope to convince the police photography expert to accompany us to demonstrate the photographic falsification technique."

Lestrade thought for a moment. "It's irregular, but given the criminal arson and the apparent scale of this fraud... Very well, Holmes. You can count on my presence. How do you plan to get me into this private session?"

Holmes smiled. "You'll be introduced as a wealthy industrialist from the North, recently returned from India and passionate about unexplained phenomena.

I've already arranged your invitation through Lady Harrington, who still believes me to be an antiquarian and is unaware of my true intentions."

"And if this Blacksmith recognizes me?"

"Unlikely. You've rarely been featured in the press, and we'll provide you with attire and an appearance that will effectively mask your identity."

Lestrade nodded, though his expression betrayed some skepticism about his acting abilities.

"One last thing," added Holmes. "I'd like to consult your records regarding criminal activities involving alleged supernatural phenomena over the past five years. Other similar cases might shed light on Blacksmith's method or reveal potential previous scams."

An hour later, after going through Scotland Yard's archives, we found ourselves in front of an elegant residence in South Kensington, Sir Edmund Blake's home. For the occasion, Holmes had adopted the persona of a scientific journalist preparing an article on modern temporal theories.

A stiff butler showed us into a vast salon whose walls were covered with bookshelves. Various scientific instruments-telescope, armillary spheres, barometers-adorned the space, giving it the atmosphere of a cabinet of intellectual curiosities.

Sir Edmund Blake kept us waiting for a few minutes before making his entrance. He was a man in his sixties, tall and thin, with an aristocratic bearing. His austere face was illuminated by bright, intelligent eyes behind gold-rimmed spectacles. The resemblance to his younger brother was undeniable, though tempered by the years and his more severe expression.

"Gentlemen," he greeted us in a measured voice, "I have little time, but I am always happy to encourage the popularization of science. Your journal is interested in temporal theories, then?"

"Indeed, Sir Edmund," replied Holmes with the slightly exaggerated enthusiasm of a journalist. "Recent discussions on the nature of time fascinate our readers. Some even go so far as to suggest the theoretical possibility of time travel."

An almost imperceptible shadow crossed Sir Edmund's gaze. "Pure fanciful speculation. No serious physicist would consider such a hypothesis."

"And yet," insisted Holmes, "I have heard of a certain Gideon Blacksmith who claims to have accomplished such a feat. His demonstrations have, so they say, impressed scientists."

The reaction was immediate but subtly controlled. Sir Edmund's fingers clenched slightly on the armrest of his chair, and tension appeared at the corners of his lips.

"I do not know this individual," he replied in an even tone. "But I can assure you that anyone claiming to travel through time is either a charlatan or mentally disturbed."

"You've never attended one of his demonstrations?" Holmes innocently asked.

"Certainly not." The answer came too quickly, almost defensively. "I occupy my time with serious research, Mr... Hardwick, is that correct?"

"Indeed. One last question, if you don't mind. What do you think of recent discoveries about electromagnetic waves? Some theorists suggest they might interact with the space-time continuum."

This question, with no apparent connection to Blacksmith, allowed Sir Edmund to regain his composure. He launched into a technical explanation where his mastery of the subject was evident. Holmes listened with an attention that, I knew, was not feigned-my friend had always shown a genuine interest in scientific advances.

When we took our leave a few minutes later, I noticed that Holmes was carefully observing the photographs adorning the corridor leading to the exit. In one of them, partially hidden behind an indoor plant, appeared two young men in university attire-Sir Edmund and his brother, no doubt, from their Oxford days.

"What do you think?" I asked once in the hansom taking us back to central London.

"Sir Edmund is lying, obviously," replied Holmes. "He knows Blacksmith perfectly well and probably follows his activities. Did you notice the slight discoloration on his right ring finger? The mark of a recently removed ring-I suspect it was an ouroboros similar to the one worn by members of the Brotherhood."

"Do you think he actively participates in the fraud?"

"I'm not certain. His discomfort was evident, but was it due to complicity or embarrassment about his brother's activities? He certainly has the scientific knowledge necessary to design devices like the 'ethereal chronometer,' but his academic status means too much to him. He wouldn't risk his reputation by openly associating with such a hoax."

Holmes reflected for a moment. "I believe it's more of a tacit arrangement. Sir Edmund turns a blind eye and indirectly benefits from the revenue generated by his brother, perhaps in the form of 'loans' or 'gifts.' In exchange, he occasionally provides indirect intellectual endorsement and technical advice."

"Our visit will have alerted him."

"That's precisely what I wanted," admitted Holmes. "I want him to warn his brother. Blacksmith will be more vigilant tonight, but also more likely to make a mistake under pressure."

The hansom stopped in front of a modest building in Camden Town. "Our last visit before tonight," announced Holmes. "I wish to speak with a certain Jeremy Foster, former photographic assistant to Bolin, who recently left his employment under interesting circumstances."

Foster's lodging consisted of a small attic room on the third floor. When he opened the door to us, I was struck by his youth-he couldn't have been more than twenty-five-and by his sickly appearance. Thin to the point of emaciation, with a pale complexion, he wore a poorly adjusted bandage on his right hand.

"Mr. Foster?" Holmes presented himself under his real name this time. "I'm investigating Mr. Geoffrey Bolin and his photographic activities."

The young man grew even paler and cast an anxious glance toward the corridor, as if fearing he was being watched.

"I have nothing to say about him," he murmured. "Nothing at all."

"Your hand," I observed with my medical instinct. "That's a chemical burn, isn't it? Poorly treated, moreover."

Foster hesitated, then slowly nodded. "A laboratory accident. With the fixing baths."

"Allow me to examine it," I offered. "I'm a doctor."

This offer seemed to reassure him. He invited us into his modestly furnished room. While I attended to his injury, Holmes began the conversation in a deliberately casual tone.

"Have you worked long for Mr. Bolin?"

"Nearly two years," replied Foster, wincing slightly as I applied antiseptic to his burn. "I started as a simple assistant, but he trained me in advanced photographic techniques."

"Including superimpositions and montages?"

The young man stiffened. "I don't know what you're talking about."

"Come now, Mr. Foster," Holmes intervened more firmly. "We've visited Bolin's workshop. We know the nature of his work, and his association with Gideon Blacksmith. You risk nothing by talking to us."

Foster remained silent while I finished bandaging his hand. Finally, as if freed from a burden, he sighed deeply.

"That's why I left," he said, pointing to his injury. "Bolin was becoming increasingly nervous, demanding overtime, making me handle caustic products without adequate protection. When I burned myself, he refused to let me see a doctor-too risky, he said."

"What exactly do you know about his activities?" asked Holmes.

"At first, it was mostly retouching work for portraits-erasing wrinkles, improving features. Then he started these... other projects. Old photographs that he modified to insert a modern person. He was obsessed with perfection, sometimes working for days on a single image."

"For Blacksmith?"

Foster nodded. "I only met him twice. A strange man, intimidating. He examined every detail, rejected any imperfect work. Once, for a simple misaligned shadow, he demanded that Bolin completely redo a montage that had taken a week of work."

Holmes took out a small notebook and pencil. "Could you describe to us, as precisely as possible, the techniques used for these falsifications?"

Foster hesitated, then, visibly relieved to finally be able to speak, explained in detail the complex processes of double exposure, fine brush retouching, and artificial aging of prints. His testimony, precise and technical, confirmed Holmes's suspicions and provided crucial details that even my friend hadn't anticipated.

"One last question," said Holmes as we prepared to leave. "Have you ever heard of a connection between Blacksmith and Sir Edmund Blake?"

"Bolin sometimes mentioned 'his contact at the Royal Society' who validated certain technical aspects of the demonstrations. I never heard a name, but..." Foster paused, seeming to remember something. "Once, I saw an envelope addressed to 'E.B.' containing a bundle of banknotes. Bolin quickly hid it when he noticed my presence."

Holmes smiled slightly. "Thank you, Mr. Foster. Your testimony could prove crucial. Would you be willing to repeat it before official representatives, if necessary?"

The young man paled again. "I... Bolin has connections. He threatened me if I talked."

"I understand your fears," said Holmes gently. "But you wouldn't be alone. Scotland Yard is already interested in this case, and your cooperation would be appreciated."

After a few moments of reflection, Foster slowly nodded. "All right. But I want guarantees for my safety."

"You'll have them," promised Holmes, handing him his card. "Be ready for tonight. An agent will come for you at seven o'clock."

Back at Baker Street, Holmes spent the afternoon meticulously organizing our evening intervention. Several telegrams were sent and received. Dr. Ainslie confirmed his presence, as did Scotland Yard's photography expert. Lestrade sent word that he had selected two experienced agents to accompany him.

At five o'clock, a voluminous package was delivered, containing the clothes and accessories intended to transform Lestrade into a wealthy industrialist from the North.

"Everything is in place, Watson," Holmes finally announced, closing his notebook. "Tonight, we shall witness the last public performance of Gideon Blacksmith, time traveler."

He settled into his armchair and lit his pipe, his face adopting that meditative expression I knew so well.

"You seem preoccupied," I remarked.

"I'm reflecting on the moral implications of this case," he replied after a moment of silence. "Blacksmith is undeniably a swindler, but a swindler of exceptional intelligence and talent. What capabilities wasted in fraud! And his victims... Some will doubtless find relief in the truth, but others will perhaps lose the only consolation they had left in the face of grief and loneliness."

"Are you hesitating to unmask him?"

Holmes vigorously shook his head. "Absolutely not. The truth is always preferable to illusion, however comfortable it may be. Moreover, Blacksmith is becoming dangerous-his stagings now involve criminal acts that could, one day, claim innocent victims."

He took a few puffs on his pipe, then added more softly: "No, what concerns me is the case of Sir Edmund Blake. A respected man of science, who has tacitly allowed his brother's fraudulent activities, perhaps out of misplaced family loyalty, perhaps out of simple greed.

His career will be irreparably tarnished when the truth comes to light."

"Perhaps he deserves that fate?" I suggested.

"Perhaps. But justice is not always served by systematic destruction, Watson. There are cases where a form of mercy may better serve society's interests than a blind application of the law."

With these enigmatic words, Holmes sank into a meditative silence that I was careful not to disturb. The sun was beginning to decline, casting long shadows in our sitting room. In a few hours, we would be confronted with one of the most elaborate and ingenious impostures we had ever encountered.

Despite Holmes's apparent assurance, I couldn't help wondering if Gideon Blacksmith, with his remarkable intelligence and considerable resources, hadn't anticipated our intervention. After all, a man capable of convincing brilliant minds that he had traveled through time was certainly not an adversary to be underestimated.

V

The evening was well advanced when we set out for Sir William Ashton's home. Holmes had insisted that we arrive separately so as not to arouse suspicion. I was to go first, followed shortly by Holmes, while Lestrade and his men, along with our experts, would appear at the appointed time, equipped with the invitations that Holmes had skillfully obtained.

"Remember, Watson," Holmes had advised me before my departure, "observe carefully but do not intervene under any circumstances before my signal. Blacksmith will be particularly vigilant tonight, and the slightest misstep could compromise everything."

The cab dropped me off in front of the imposing residence whose brilliantly lit windows contrasted with the surrounding darkness. A light drizzle was falling, enveloping the streetlamps in a ghostly halo that accentuated the strange atmosphere of the evening.

Lady Harrington welcomed me in the entrance hall, visibly delighted by my presence. "Dr. Watson! What a joy to see you again. Mr. Sherrinford isn't with you?"

"He'll join us shortly," I replied. "An urgent matter detained him."

"Perfect. You arrive at just the right moment. Tonight is a particularly important session-Mr. Blacksmith has promised us an exceptional demonstration of his faculties."

She led me to the library, transformed for the occasion into an even more theatrical space than during our previous visit. Heavy purple curtains had been drawn over the windows, silver candelabra dispensed a subdued light, and a more elaborate stage had been erected at one end of the room. On it stood the famous "ethereal chronometer," more imposing than I remembered, surrounded by several other devices whose function escaped me.

About twenty people were already present, conversing in hushed tones with that contained excitement typical of initiates about to share a rare privilege. I noticed that almost all now wore the ring with the ouroboros emblem, a sign of their membership in the Brotherhood.

Sir William Ashton came to greet me, his face animated with an almost religious fervor. "Dr. Watson, welcome! Mr. Blacksmith confided to me that he appreciated your presence at the last session-your medical skepticism, he says, is exactly the type of mind he wishes to convince."

I endeavored to appear flattered while discreetly observing the new arrivals. Among them was a corpulent man with a graying beard and ostentatious clothing whom I barely recognized as Lestrade. His transformation was remarkable-false sideburns, tinted glasses, and a skillfully adjusted wig had completely altered his appearance.

Beside him stood a thin man with an austere face whom I guessed to be Dr. Ainslie. A third individual carrying a case that probably contained photographic equipment completed the group-the Scotland Yard expert, presumably.

Holmes made his entrance shortly after, greeting several people with ease as if he had known them for a long time. His talent for social infiltration never ceased to amaze me. He gave me an imperceptible nod before engaging in an animated conversation with Lord Pembrooke.

At eight o'clock precisely, the doors of the library were closed and the lights further dimmed, leaving only the stage illuminated. An expectant silence settled as Sir William Ashton stepped forward to introduce the session.

"My dear friends, members of the Brotherhood," he began solemnly, "tonight marks an important milestone in our journey toward understanding the mysteries of time. Our guide, Mr. Blacksmith, honors us with an exceptional demonstration that will, I am certain, dispel the last doubts of the most skeptical among us."

A murmur of approval ran through the audience. Sir William continued:

"As you know, many of us have already benefited from extraordinary personal evidence of his abilities. Tonight, however, Mr. Blacksmith has agreed to share certain aspects of his science that until now were reserved for initiates of the inner circle."

I spotted Holmes who, from his corner of the room, was carefully scrutinizing the reactions of the various members. His gaze lingered particularly on a figure who had just discreetly entered through a side door and taken a seat in the last row-a man I hadn't immediately noticed but whom I recognized, with surprise, as Sir Edmund Blake.

"And now," Sir William concluded with a theatrical gesture, "I have the honor of presenting to you the man who has crossed the barriers of time, Mr. Gideon Blacksmith!"

A door opened at the back of the stage, and Blacksmith appeared in a halo of bluish light produced by an ingenious electrical device. His attire differed from what he had worn during our previous encounter-he now sported an impeccable period costume that would have seemed perfectly at home in a salon of 1820. Around his neck gleamed a silver medallion depicting an ouroboros more elaborate than those worn by his disciples.

"My friends," he began in a measured voice that carried to the back of the room without ever seeming forced, "I thank you for your presence tonight. Some of you have been here since the beginning of my journey in your era. Others join us with a fresh perspective, perhaps skeptical-and I commend them for it."

His gaze swept across the audience and paused briefly on Holmes, then on Lestrade, before continuing:

"Skepticism is the guardian of truth. Without it, we would sink into superstition or blind credulity. That is why I have always encouraged critical examination of my claims."

I had to admit that his eloquence was remarkable, his stage presence undeniable. Even knowing it was an imposture, I couldn't help being impressed by the conviction that emanated from this man.

"Tonight," he continued, "I wish to offer you three demonstrations of the reality of time travel. Not to convince you-for true conviction must come from within-but to invite you to consider possibilities beyond the limits that conventional science imposes upon itself."

He approached the ethereal chronometer and activated it with a precise gesture. The device gradually illuminated, emitting a deep hum that seemed to make the very air vibrate. Bluish electrical arcs sprang between different parts of the mechanism, creating a spectacle as unsettling as it was fascinating.

"What you observe is merely the visible manifestation of an infinitely more complex phenomenon," explained Blacksmith as the apparatus reached its optimal operation. "The ethereal oscillations generated by this device create a local disturbance in the very fabric of time, allowing the establishment of a limited temporal corridor."

At these words, a strange phenomenon occurred. The space around the chronometer seemed to distort slightly, as if the air became viscous. A small object placed on a pedestal beside the device-a pocket watch, I noticed-began to vibrate and then to move without anything seemingly touching it.

Muffled exclamations rose from the audience. I observed Holmes, who was examining the scene with intense concentration, his eyes moving from the chronometer to the floor and then to the ceiling, as if searching for something specific.

"What you have just observed," Blacksmith resumed once the device had calmed, "is the effect of a disturbed temporal field on a contemporary object. The watch you see momentarily existed simultaneously in two different temporalities, creating this apparent levitation."

He made a calculated pause before adding: "But let us now move on to a more personal demonstration."

Blacksmith took from his pocket a small polished wooden box which he opened with care. Inside was what appeared to be a lock of hair wrapped in a faded ribbon.

"Lady Harrington," he said, turning to our hostess, "may I ask you to confirm to the assembly what I revealed to you during our private conversation regarding your late husband?"

Lady Harrington stood up, visibly moved. "Mr. Blacksmith described to me with absolute precision the sapphire brooch that my husband had given me, which he could not have known through any conventional means. He also..." her voice trembled slightly, "he also conveyed a personal message that only Henry could have known."

"Indeed," confirmed Blacksmith. "And tonight, I have something to give you."

He handed her the box. "This hair belonged to Judge Harrington. In my original temporality, I briefly crossed his path in 1822, when he was only a promising young jurist. He entrusted me with this locket containing a lock of his hair, intended for his future wife-a romantic tradition of the time. Circumstances prevented him from ever giving it to her."

Lady Harrington, with trembling hands, took the box and examined it with palpable emotion. "It's... it's his handwriting on the ribbon," she whispered. "The same initials he used in his personal letters."

I saw several members of the audience exchange impressed looks. The emotional effect was undeniable.

Even Lestrade, despite his disguise, seemed troubled by the scene.

Holmes, however, observed the scene with increased intensity. I saw him discreetly note something in a small notebook.

"My third demonstration," continued Blacksmith, "concerns a future event. As some of you already know, my temporal crossing generated an unexpected side effect-a limited ability to perceive fragments of upcoming events."

He took out a sealed envelope which he handed to Sir William. "I have recorded here a vision I had last night. I suggest you keep it sealed until its realization, probably within two days."

Sir William took the envelope with reverence, but before he could put it away, a voice rose from the back of the room.

"Wouldn't it be more convincing to reveal this prediction immediately?"

All eyes turned to Holmes, who had stood up and was slowly approaching the stage. Blacksmith stared at him with an inscrutable expression.

"Mr. Sherrinford, isn't it? Your skepticism is understandable, but visions don't work on demand."

"Are you certain about that?" replied Holmes, suddenly abandoning his antiquarian persona. "Because it seems to me that your 'visions' have thus far obeyed a remarkably precise and opportune schedule."

A surprised murmur ran through the assembly. Blacksmith maintained his composure, though slight tension appeared on his face.

"I don't understand you, sir."

"Allow me to be clearer," replied Holmes as he reached the stage. "I am not Mr. Sherrinford the antiquarian, but Sherlock Holmes, consulting detective. And I am here to end an imposture that has gone on long enough."

The silence that followed this declaration was almost palpable. Blacksmith, after a moment of apparent surprise, smiled slightly.

"Mr. Holmes. Your reputation precedes you. I'm flattered that you consider my work worthy of your attention, but I fear you're mistaken."

"Am I so sure?" Holmes retorted. Then, turning to the audience: "Ladies and gentlemen, tonight I propose an alternative demonstration-that of the methods used by Mr. Blacksmith to create the illusion of time travel."

Holmes made a discreet gesture, and Lestrade stood up, removing his tinted glasses and false sideburns. "Inspector Lestrade, Scotland Yard," he announced, provoking a new wave of murmurs.

"With Sir William's kind permission," Holmes continued, "I have invited a few experts who will enlighten us about our time traveler's 'miracles.'"

Sir William, visibly disconcerted, seemed about to protest, but Lady Harrington placed a calming hand on his arm. "Let's allow Mr. Holmes to speak. If Mr. Blacksmith speaks the truth, he has nothing to fear."

Holmes nodded in thanks. "Let's begin with this 'ethereal chronometer,' the centerpiece of this deception."

He approached the device and, without hesitation, bent down to examine its base. "As I suspected," he said, straightening up. "An electromagnetic device powered by batteries concealed under the stage. The luminous effects are produced by an ingenious combination of controlled electrical discharges and metallic salts. As for the 'levitation' of this watch..."

Holmes stooped and pulled on an almost invisible wire that connected the object to a mechanism hidden in the draperies. "A simple conjuring trick, using a magnet and a black silk thread."

Blacksmith kept his composure, but I saw a vein pulsing at his temple. "Simplistic accusations, Mr. Holmes. Electromagnetism is merely a minor component of the chronometer, used to stabilize the ethereal vortex."

"Really?" Holmes beckoned Dr. Ainslie to approach. "Allow me to introduce Dr. Ainslie, chemist at Imperial College. Doctor, tell us about the journal fragment I submitted for your analysis."

Dr. Ainslie stepped forward, holding a report which he presented to the assembly. "I analyzed a sample of Mr. Blacksmith's alleged 1824 journal. The paper contains wood fibers treated by an industrial process that did not exist before 1860. The ink contains traces of aniline black, a synthetic pigment discovered in 1863. This document absolutely cannot date from the claimed period."

Exclamations of surprise were heard. I saw several members of the Brotherhood exchange troubled glances.

"Now let's move on to the photograph," Holmes continued, signaling to the Scotland Yard expert. "Mr. Blacksmith presented us with a daguerreotype supposedly showing him in 1843. Here is Mr. Parker, specialist in forensic photography, who will explain how this 'evidence' was fabricated."

The expert opened his case and took out several photographic plates and instruments. "The technique used is known as superimposition. It consists of combining two negatives to create a composite image. I was able to examine the original photograph without Mr. Blacksmith, and here is the result of my analysis."

He projected two images onto a screen using a magic lantern: the photograph shown by Blacksmith, and the same scene without his presence.

"As you can see, the original image has been modified to insert Mr. Blacksmith. The shadows don't match perfectly, and microscopic analysis reveals traces of fine brush retouching around his silhouette."

The unease in the room was now palpable. Several people stood up, visibly disoriented by these revelations. Lady Harrington, for her part, stared intensely at Blacksmith, her expression oscillating between disbelief and nascent anger.

Holmes wasn't finished. "As for our friend's remarkably precise 'predictions,' they deserve special explanation." He took from his pocket the clockwork mechanism recovered after the fire. "This device was used to trigger the Billingsgate warehouse fire, exactly at the time 'predicted' by Mr. Blacksmith. It was abandoned by his accomplice, a certain Geoffrey Bolin, whom Inspector Lestrade is currently searching for on charges of criminal arson."

Blacksmith, who had maintained a facade of disdainful calm until then, began to show signs of agitation. "These accusations are absurd. You have no tangible proof of what you're claiming."

"On the contrary," replied Holmes. "I visited the Camden Town workshop where your accomplice Bolin creates his photographic falsifications and manufactures your 'ethereal' devices. There I found detailed files on each of your victims-pardon me, your 'disciples'-with all the personal information necessary to create the illusion of supernatural knowledge."

He turned to Lady Harrington. "Madam, the sapphire brooch that Blacksmith described so precisely appears in a photograph displayed at your son's home, Lieutenant Harrington. As for this box supposedly containing a lock of your late husband's hair..."

Holmes approached and examined it briefly. "The ribbon is indeed old, but it has been recently manipulated. The handwriting has been carefully imitated from samples available in your family archives, to which Blake gained access during a visit to your son, presenting himself as a researcher in legal history."

Lady Harrington brought a trembling hand to her mouth, her eyes filling with tears.

"Ladies and gentlemen," Holmes concluded, "you have been victims of an elaborate fraud. Mr. Gideon Blacksmith is not a time traveler, but Garrett Blake, born in 1855 in Cambridge, son of Professor Harold Blake, a historian specializing in the Georgian period-which explains his remarkable knowledge of obscure historical details."

At this revelation, Blacksmith-or rather Blake-seemed to finally lose his composure. His face contorted with fury, and in a sudden movement, he attempted to rush toward the rear exit.

"Stop him!" cried Lestrade.

Two plainclothes officers who had positioned themselves near the exits intercepted Blake before he could escape. He struggled for a moment, then, realizing the futility of his resistance, straightened up with recovered dignity.

"You think you've won, Holmes," he hissed through his teeth. "But you have no idea what you're destroying. These people," he indicated the audience with a sweeping gesture, "found in my teachings a hope, a transcendence that your materialistic world denies them. What do you offer in exchange? The emptiness of an existence without mystery!"

"I offer the truth," Holmes replied calmly. "However harsh it may sometimes be."

The room was now in a state of total confusion. Some Brotherhood members seemed devastated, others furious; a few were hastily leaving the premises. Lestrade approached Blake to formally proceed with his arrest.

It was then that a voice rose from the back of the room. "One moment, please."

Sir Edmund Blake stepped forward, his usually austere face marked by profound weariness. "Inspector, before proceeding, may I speak briefly with Mr. Holmes and... my brother?"

Lestrade hesitated, then acquiesced after a nod from Holmes. "Five minutes, no more."

The two brothers and Holmes withdrew to an adjacent room, while I helped Lestrade maintain a semblance of order among the disoriented guests. Lady Harrington, in particular, seemed devastated, staring at the box containing the supposed lock of her husband's hair as if contemplating the ruins of her last hopes.

When Holmes returned a few minutes later, his expression was inscrutable. Without a word to me, he addressed the assembly:

"Ladies and gentlemen, I ask for your attention for one more moment. This case has complex ramifications. Mr. Garrett Blake will be prosecuted for fraud and criminal arson, but certain considerations must be taken into account."

He glanced toward Sir Edmund, who nodded imperceptibly.

"Sir Edmund Blake, whose scientific reputation is at stake, commits to fully reimburse all sums paid to the Brotherhood of Ethereal Travelers. In exchange, I hope you will consider the private aspect of this matter and avoid a public scandal that would serve no one."

A murmur ran through the audience, but no one openly protested. Holmes's proposal, although surprising, offered an elegant way out of a potentially embarrassing situation for all.

Lestrade, after consulting his notes, announced: "Mr. Blake will be taken away discreetly. Those wishing to file a formal complaint can contact me tomorrow at Scotland Yard. The others are free to leave."

The evening ended in a surreal atmosphere, with guests leaving in silent small groups. I saw Sir Edmund approach Lady Harrington and speak to her in a low voice, probably to apologize and discuss the reimbursement arrangements.

Holmes and I were among the last to leave. On the mansion's steps, while waiting for a hansom, I turned to my friend:

"What happened in that room with the Blake brothers?"

Holmes lit his pipe and contemplated the smoke swirls rising into the now-clear night. "An arrangement, Watson. Sir Edmund admitted to turning a blind eye to his brother's activities and indirectly profiting from them. In exchange for his cooperation and full reimbursement of the victims, I agreed not to publicly expose his involvement."

"Is that really just?" I asked, somewhat troubled by this compromise.

"Justice sometimes takes unexpected forms," Holmes replied. "Sir Edmund will quietly resign from his position at the Royal Society. His scientific career is effectively over, but his name won't be dragged through the mud. As for Garrett, he will pay for his crimes, particularly the arson which could have had much more serious consequences."

Our hansom arrived, and we boarded in silence. As we crossed the London streets, Holmes added, almost to himself:

"What fascinates me about this case is the extraordinary power of suggestion and the desire to believe. Men and women of education and reason accepted the impossible because it offered a consolation that reality denied them. Blake understood this and exploited it with diabolical skill."

"And now that the illusion is dispelled?"

Holmes shrugged. "Some will find other beliefs to fill their void, others will perhaps finally confront their grief and fears. But all, I hope, will be more wary of too-comfortable certainties."

The rest of the journey passed in meditative silence. I couldn't help thinking about Lady Harrington and her lost sapphire brooch, symbol of a bygone happiness that no time traveler, real or imaginary, could ever return to her.

VI

Several weeks passed before the last echoes of the Blacksmith affair faded away. The press made only limited mention of it, referring to the arrest of a "high-class swindler" without delving into compromising details about the members of the defunct Brotherhood. This relative discretion was largely due to Lord Pembrooke's influence over several London newspapers-his way, no doubt, of preventing his own credulity from becoming a topic of conversation in the clubs of Pall Mall.

Holmes, absorbed in new investigations, seemed to have relegated the affair to the compartment of his memory reserved for solved cases. It was only on a rainy December evening, when the wind howled through the chimneys of Baker Street with mournful whistles, that the subject resurfaced.

I had just finished reading The Times and was preparing to retire when Holmes, who had spent the afternoon sorting his correspondence, handed me a letter.

"Read this, Watson. It's from Lestrade."

The missive, written in the inspector's characteristic administrative style, informed me that Garrett Blake had been sentenced to five years of hard labor for fraud and criminal arson. His accomplice Geoffrey Bolin had received a reduced sentence in exchange for his cooperation with justice.

"And what about Sir Edmund?" I asked, returning the letter to Holmes.

"He kept his word." Holmes puffed on his pipe, contemplating the dancing flames in the fireplace. "All Brotherhood members have been fully reimbursed. Sir Edmund sold his Kensington property and resigned from his position at the Royal Society, citing failing health. He now lives in a modest property in Devonshire, where he pursues private research."

"A lenient fate, considering his complicity."

"Perhaps." Holmes joined his fingertips beneath his chin in that meditative gesture so familiar to him. "But don't forget that his active participation was never formally established. He certainly turned a blind eye, perhaps accepted money from his brother, but he never directly participated in the sessions or the swindles."

"A subtle distinction," I remarked.

"Life is made of such nuances, my dear Watson. Between the black of crime and the white of innocence extends a vast grey area where the law struggles to define precise boundaries. It is sometimes in these interstices that true justice must find its way."

Holmes rose and went to the window. Outside, London was disappearing under a curtain of rain, the streetlamps offering only ghostly halos in the winter mist.

"I received another communication that might interest you," he said, returning to his armchair. "From Lady Harrington."

"How is she recovering from this affair?"

"Better than one might expect." Holmes smiled slightly. "She writes to inform me that she has decided to use the funds restored by Sir Edmund to create a foundation that will finance rigorous scientific research on unexplained phenomena."

"That's unexpected!"

"Not so much. Lady Harrington possesses a remarkable intelligence and training in mathematics that she has too long neglected. This affair, though painful, seems to have awakened her interest in methodical investigation."

Holmes leaned forward and added a log to the fire. The flames revived, projecting our enlarged shadows on the papered walls.

"There's something profoundly revealing about this case, Watson," he continued after a moment of silence. "We demonstrated that Blacksmith was an impostor, that his evidence was falsified, that his predictions were orchestrated. And yet..."

"And yet?" I encouraged him, surprised by his unusual hesitation.

"And yet, we haven't answered the fundamental question that haunted his disciples: is it possible to transcend the limits of our temporal existence? Blake's fraud doesn't invalidate the quest itself."

"You surprise me, Holmes. I didn't know you were inclined to metaphysical speculation."

He gave a short laugh. "Don't misunderstand me, my friend. I remain firmly anchored in the material world of observable facts. But I've learned to recognize that the need to believe in something that exceeds our immediate experience is a constant of human nature."

"Like the belief in an afterlife where we would be reunited with our loved ones?"

"Precisely. Lady Harrington and the others weren't merely victims of a financial scam. They were stripped of a consolation, a hope. Blake understood this fundamental need and exploited it with diabolical skill."

I pondered these words while listening to the crackling of the fire and the drumming of rain against the windowpanes. Holmes seemed absorbed in his own reflections, his gaze fixed on an invisible point.

"Do you know what troubled me most in this entire affair?" he suddenly resumed. "It's that Blake, despite his undeniable genius, chose the path of fraud rather than legitimate creation. With his historical erudition, his technical ingenuity, and his theatrical talent, he could have truly contributed to the advancement of knowledge."

"What drives a man to misuse his gifts in such a way?" I asked.

"A fascinating question, my dear Watson." Holmes leaned back in his chair, his eyes half-closed. "Perhaps we'll find a clue in his very choice of deception: time travel. Isn't it revealing of a desire to escape his era, his identity perhaps? Garrett Blake, younger son of a respected historian, living in the shadow of a brilliant older brother, disgraced by an academic scandal... he reinvented himself as Gideon Blacksmith, a mysterious figure from an idealized past."

"A form of escape, then?"

"Or revenge. By becoming Blacksmith, he created an existence where he dominated those very people who would have despised him as Blake-aristocrats, intellectuals, authority figures. He played with them like a puppeteer with his dolls."

The clock struck midnight, its twelve strokes resonating in our cozy sitting room. Holmes rose to revive the fire one last time.

"Time, Watson," he said almost to himself. "That's the true enigma that neither science nor fraud can fully comprehend. We move inexorably in its current, unable to go backward to correct our mistakes or relive our joys. Is it any wonder that the idea of breaking free from it exerts such fascination?"

"You almost speak as if you envied Blake his chimera," I observed with a smile.

Holmes laughed briefly. "Not at all. The appeal of time travel lies in its theory, not in its illusory practice. The mysteries of the present amply suffice for me, and the past, though physically inaccessible, reveals its secrets through the clues it leaves behind."

He stretched and yawned slightly. "It's getting late, my friend. Tomorrow awaits us with a busy day-this blackmail case in the Danish royal family promises to be stimulating."

As I rose to retire, a question crossed my mind. "Holmes, do you think Blake believed, even a little, in his own stories? Could he, by playing the role of Blacksmith for so long, have come to identify with this character?"

Holmes considered the question carefully. "An intriguing hypothesis. Great impostors often end up inhabiting their lies so fully that the boundary between reality and fiction blurs in their minds. Blake may have begun with full awareness of his fraud, but after years of living as Blacksmith..." He let his sentence trail off, contemplating the last embers in the hearth.

"Good night, Watson," he finally said. "May your dreams carry you to kinder times than our foggy present."

THE CASE OF THE MISSING AIRSHIP

I

It was one of those rainy March afternoons when London seems wrapped in a mantle of grayness. The fine, incessant rain streamed down the windows of 221B Baker Street, and the crackling of the fire in the hearth brought a welcome comfort to the dreary atmosphere. Seated in my usual armchair, I was absently leafing through the pages of a recent medical journal, while my companion, Sherlock Holmes, was absorbed in one of his chemical experiments.

On the table before him lay a small metallic fragment that he was examining with the aid of his microscope. From time to time, he would dip a delicate brush into a vial containing a clear liquid and apply a drop to the metal, carefully observing the reactions. His lean, angular face was illuminated by the flickering light of a gas lamp, and his eyes shone with an almost disturbing intensity.

"Fascinating, Watson," he said suddenly without raising his eyes from his work. "This alloy fragment is not only remarkably light, but it also possesses exceptional strength. Imagine the possible applications in the field of transportation!"

I made an effort to appear interested, though I had never shared his enthusiasm for technical sciences. "And where does this sample come from?" I asked.

"From a most intriguing industrial project," he replied, finally straightening up. "But I shall tell you more in due time. For now, I can state that this alloy could revolutionize our era."

Before I could respond, Holmes raised a hand to silence me. He cocked his ear and sketched an enigmatic smile.

"We are about to have company," he declared.

Hardly had he spoken these words when heavy footsteps resounded on the staircase leading to our apartment. A moment later, the door opened to reveal the massive, imposing figure of Mycroft Holmes. My admiration for Sherlock was equaled only by my fascination with his elder brother, whose analytical mind surpassed even the detective's in certain domains.

"Good day, Sherlock," said Mycroft, entering without ceremony. "Watson."

He set his dripping umbrella in a corner and sat heavily in the vacant armchair near the fire. His broad, pale face wore a grave expression that left no doubt about the importance of his visit.

"I suppose you are here on a matter of state," Sherlock remarked with a wry smile.

Mycroft nodded. "A most serious matter. An experimental airship has disappeared during a test flight over the Norfolk marshes."

I couldn't help reacting with surprise. "An airship?"

"Yes, Watson," replied Mycroft, casting me a penetrating look. "But not just any airship. This prototype was designed by Sir Edward Hawthorne, a man whose scientific genius is as great as his political ambitions are controversial. This airship represents a major technological advancement for our country-or for any other that might seize it."

Sherlock sat up in his chair, visibly interested. "And what are the exact circumstances of this disappearance?"

Mycroft took out a file he had brought and placed it on the table before us. "The airship took off three days ago from a private base belonging to Hawthorne Industries. It was to perform a simple circular flight above the marshes before returning to its starting point. However, it never returned, and no trace has been found since."

Holmes opened the file and quickly perused the documents it contained: technical diagrams of the airship, meteorological observation reports, and testimonies from staff members present at takeoff.

"Fascinating," he murmured, examining one of the diagrams. "This lifting gas mentioned here-is it an invention of Dr. Ellen Loxley?"

Mycroft nodded approvingly. "Exactly. A brilliant chemist who has been working for Hawthorne Industries for several years. She developed this revolutionary gas that allows the airship to float with unmatched efficiency."

Holmes closed the file and turned to his brother with a piercing gaze.

"And why come to me? You certainly have competent men in the government to handle this kind of affair..."

Mycroft sighed deeply before responding: "Because this case exceeds the usual competencies of official forces. There are too many troubling elements-inconsistencies in testimonies, disturbing rumors about Hawthorne himself... And above all because if this technology were to fall into the wrong hands, the consequences could be disastrous for our country and beyond."

Sherlock remained silent for a few moments, tapping his fingers against the arm of his chair.

"Very well," he finally said, rising abruptly. "Watson, prepare your notebook-we have an investigation to conduct!"

Mycroft stayed with us for another half hour, providing all the details he had regarding the missing airship. The plans he had brought revealed a truly remarkable machine, a device that could have radically transformed British aerial transport and military applications.

"This airship," he explained, "represents the culmination of five years of intensive research. Sir Edward Hawthorne has invested not only his personal fortune but has also obtained considerable funds from several ministries, all convinced of the project's strategic value."

Holmes studied the documents meticulously, his piercing eyes missing no detail.

"And what makes this airship so special compared to existing models?" I asked.

"Two major innovations, Watson," replied Mycroft before his brother could. "First, an extraordinarily light yet resistant metal alloy, developed by Hawthorne himself. Second, a revolutionary lifting gas, far more efficient than hydrogen, designed by Dr. Ellen Loxley, a brilliant chemist who works for Hawthorne."

"And no one saw this airship crash? No trace has been found?" asked Holmes.

"Nothing. A thick fog had risen over the marshes that day. The airship simply disappeared into the mist."

Holmes rose abruptly, a spark of excitement in his eyes. "We must go immediately to Hawthorne Industries. Mycroft, could you provide us with a letter of introduction?"

An hour later, we were riding in a cab toward London's eastern outskirts, where numerous modern factories had developed. Holmes was silent, his gaze lost outside, but I knew from experience that his mind was working at a prodigious speed, already considering various hypotheses.

Hawthorne Industries occupied a vast complex of imposing buildings, dominated by tall chimneys from which gray smoke billowed. The red brick walls appeared to have been recently constructed, testifying to the company's rapid expansion. Workers came and went through a large gate surmounted by the Hawthorne family crest: a raven holding a branch of thorns in its beak.

The guard at the entrance led us through a paved courtyard to an elegant administrative building. There, we were greeted by a tall man with broad shoulders and an angular face framed by a carefully trimmed salt-and-pepper beard. His steel-blue eyes scrutinized us intensely.

"Gentlemen, I am Sir Edward Hawthorne. What can I do for you?"

Holmes presented Mycroft's letter, all while carefully observing our host. "We are investigating the disappearance of your airship, Sir Edward. I hope you can enlighten us about the exact circumstances of this incident."

Hawthorne's face remained impassive, but I thought I detected slight tension in his jaw. "Of course, Mr. Holmes. I am at the complete disposal of Her Majesty's government. Follow me, I'll show you our facilities."

He led us through workshops where workers busied themselves with various metal structures. The smell of heated metal and chemicals filled the air. Impressive machines shaped plates of a silvery metal that seemed extraordinarily light.

"Here is our special alloy," explained Hawthorne with evident pride. "Three times lighter than steel, but almost as strong. A revolution in aeronautical construction."

Holmes paused to examine a plate, weighing it with interest. "Fascinating. And is this material of your invention?"

"Yes. The fruit of twenty years of research."

We continued our tour to a modern chemical laboratory where several assistants worked before complex apparatus. It was there that we met Dr. Ellen

Loxley, a woman in her thirties with fine, intelligent features. Her brown hair was severely pulled back, and her green eyes expressed a keen intelligence, but also a certain anxiety that she tried to conceal.

"Dr. Loxley is our chief chemist," Hawthorne introduced. "She developed the gas that allows our airship to rise into the air with unmatched efficiency."

"It is an honor to meet you, Mr. Holmes," she said, shaking his hand. "I have read with great interest your methods of chemical analysis in Dr. Watson's medical journal."

Holmes inclined his head slightly. "I would be curious to learn more about your lifting gas, doctor. What are its exact properties?"

I noticed that Hawthorne had stiffened slightly at this question.

"Dr. Loxley is bound by a very strict confidentiality agreement," he promptly intervened. "But just know that this gas offers 40% greater lift than hydrogen, while being much less flammable."

Holmes nodded, but I saw that he had noted Hawthorne's hasty intervention. His eyes turned to Dr. Loxley, who slightly lowered her gaze.

Our visit continued to a vast hangar, now empty, where the airship had been assembled. Holmes asked many technical questions about the vessel, the composition of the crew, and the details of the test flight. Hawthorne's answers seemed precise and professional, but I knew my friend well enough to sense that he was not entirely satisfied.

Just then, a tall man entered the hangar. His bearing was that of a military man, straight and assured. His severe face bore a scar that crossed his left cheek, and I immediately noticed his right hand, gloved in an articulated metal case that gleamed under the hangar light.

"Ah, here is Jonas Crayle, my head of security," announced Hawthorne. "Crayle, this is Mr. Sherlock Holmes and Dr. Watson. They're investigating the disappearance of the airship."

The man observed us with a cold, calculating gaze, lingering particularly on Holmes. His handshake was firm, almost painful, the pressure of his metal hand deliberately intimidating.

"Ironhand Crayle, as they call me," he said in a gruff voice. "I'm responsible for the security of all Hawthorne facilities."

"A former military man, I presume?" asked Holmes.

"66th Infantry Regiment. Afghanistan campaign." His response was brief, almost hostile.

I shuddered slightly. I had served as a military surgeon in Afghanistan myself, and I wondered if our paths had crossed in that distant theater of operations.

"Your hand..." I began.

"An industrial accident, three years ago," Hawthorne cut in. "Crayle was supervising the installation of a new machine. Since then, he's worn this prosthesis of our design."

Holmes observed the metal hand with undisguised interest. "A remarkable piece of engineering. It seems to offer almost natural dexterity."

A flash of pride crossed Crayle's gaze. "It serves me well, sir."

As we continued our tour, I noticed that Holmes was carefully observing Hawthorne. At one point, he stopped suddenly, pretending to examine a document, but I saw that his gaze was fixed on the industrialist's cuff.

Later, as Hawthorne moved away to fetch documents related to the test flight, Holmes leaned toward me.

"Watson," he murmured, "did you notice that stain on our host's right cuff?"

"A stain? No, I didn't see anything particular."

"A very specific chemical residue. I've observed it before in my experiments on incapacitating compounds. It's not the kind of substance one would handle in developing a simple lifting gas."

Before I could respond, Hawthorne returned with several documents which he presented to us. Holmes perused them quickly, asking precise questions about each technical aspect, but I sensed that he was concealing his true concerns behind this façade of scientific interest.

At the end of our visit, Holmes courteously thanked our host. "Your explanations have been most enlightening, Sir Edward. I thank you for your time."

"Did you obtain the information you were seeking?" asked Hawthorne.

An enigmatic smile formed on Holmes's lips. "Let's say I've gathered some most interesting elements. We will probably need to return to complete our investigation."

We took our leave and climbed back into our cab. It was only when we were at a good distance that Holmes broke his silence.

"This case is far more complex than it appears, Watson. We are facing a most troubling mystery."

"Do you have a theory?" I asked.

"I have exactly seventeen at the moment," he replied, puffing on his pipe. "But to validate them, we shall have to deepen our research. Upon our return to Baker Street, I'll need to consult certain chemical texts and examine these samples I discreetly collected."

I looked at him with surprise. "You collected samples?"

A mischievous smile illuminated his austere face. "Obviously, my dear Watson. A detective should never leave a potential scene without taking some material evidence."

And thus truly began our investigation into the strange case of the Hawthorne airship.

II

Back at our Baker Street apartment, Holmes rushed to his bookshelf and pulled out several volumes devoted to modern chemistry. He arranged them on his work table, then took from his pocket a carefully folded handkerchief containing various samples collected during our visit: a fragment of the light metal, a tiny vial of dust gathered from the laboratory floor, and what I assumed to be residue from Hawthorne's cuff.

"You hardly seem convinced by our host's explanations," I observed as he prepared his analytical instruments.

"It's not so much what he said that intrigues me, Watson, but rather what he took great care to omit," he replied, placing a sample under his microscope. "Did you notice Dr. Loxley's expression when Hawthorne interrupted her?"

"She seemed uncomfortable."

"Precisely! A brilliant woman of science, silenced by her employer just as she was about to speak of her own invention. And that's not the only troubling detail. This Jonas Crayle, for instance, with his metal glove..."

"An unpleasant individual," I said, shuddering at the memory of his steel grip. "Do you think he played a role in the airship's disappearance?"

Holmes didn't respond immediately, absorbed in examining the sample. After a few minutes of silence, he straightened abruptly.

"Fascinating! This stain on Hawthorne's cuff contains traces of a very particular organic arsenic compound. A derivative of cacodylate, if I'm not mistaken."

"Arsenic?" I exclaimed with concern. "A poison?"

"Not necessarily in this form and concentration," replied Holmes, consulting one of his books. "But mixed with other substances... Ah, this is interesting."

He leapt up and headed to his archive trunk. After rummaging frantically, he pulled out a bundle of newspaper clippings yellowed with time.

"I knew this name sounded familiar. About eight years ago, when you were still in Afghanistan, my dear Watson, I followed with interest the work of a certain Dr. Harrington on volatile arsenic compounds. His research was abruptly interrupted after an accident in his laboratory caused the death of two assistants."

He handed me a clipping relating the incident in question.

"And what connection does this have with our case?" I asked.

"Dr. Harrington had one principal patron: Sir Edward Hawthorne. And guess who was his laboratory assistant who miraculously survived the accident?"

"Dr. Ellen Loxley?"

"Exactly!" exclaimed Holmes, rubbing his hands with excitement. "The connection is established. And there's more..."

He immersed himself in his research while I lit the lamps, night falling rapidly over London. For more than two hours, Holmes examined his samples, consulted various books, and scribbled frantic notes. I knew him too well to interrupt his concentration, merely bringing him an occasional cup of tea which he completely ignored.

Finally, around eleven in the evening, he dropped into his armchair and lit his pipe, his gaze lost in the swirls of smoke.

"I believe I'm beginning to see clearly, Watson," he murmured. "The airship didn't disappear by accident. It was deliberately diverted."

"By Hawthorne himself? But to what end?"

"Ah, that's the real question!" Holmes drew a long puff from his pipe. "My chemical research confirms my suspicions: the gas developed by Dr. Loxley could have other properties besides simply lifting an airship. Modified with certain arsenic compounds, it could become an extremely effective incapacitating agent."

"You're suggesting a chemical weapon?" I exclaimed, horrified by the idea.

"It's a possibility we cannot dismiss." Holmes rose abruptly and went to his desk. "I've also done some research on our metal-handed friend. Jonas Crayle didn't lose his hand in an industrial accident, as Hawthorne claims."

He handed me a military document.

"Sergeant Jonas Crayle was stricken from the military roster five years ago following an incident involving Afghan prisoners. His hand was mutilated during an explosion that he himself allegedly orchestrated to eliminate troublesome witnesses. The affair was hushed up, but he was nevertheless dismissed from his duties."

"Good God!"

"And that's not all," continued Holmes, taking another document from his desk. "I sent a telegram to my brother Mycroft regarding certain associations to which Hawthorne might belong. His response has just arrived."

He handed me the telegram, and I read aloud:

"Hawthorne founding member discreet society named Promethean League. Secret meetings. Influential members. Disturbing ideology based on scientific and intellectual superiority. To be watched closely."

Holmes nodded gravely. "Mythology teaches us that Prometheus stole fire from the gods to give to men. An appropriate symbol for someone who might see himself as a benefactor to humanity... or at least to a certain portion of humanity he would deem worthy of his gifts."

A shiver ran down my spine. "What do you intend to do now?"

"Tomorrow, we shall go to the Norfolk marshes. I want to examine for myself the place where the airship supposedly disappeared." Holmes consulted his watch. "It's late, my friend. I suggest you get some rest. Tomorrow promises to be exhausting."

When I came down for breakfast the next morning, I found Holmes already dressed and ready to depart, consulting the train timetables.

"Ah, Watson! I hope you've packed for at least one night. The train to Norwich leaves in an hour, and from there we'll have to hire a carriage to reach the marshes."

Once settled in our first-class compartment, Holmes remained silent for a long while, observing the passing landscape, London's suburbs gradually giving way to the green countryside of Suffolk. I knew from experience it was useless to disturb him in his reflections, and I immersed myself in reading The Times.

It wasn't until after we had passed Cambridge that he finally broke his silence.

"Did you know, Watson, that Sir Edward Hawthorne is considered one of the most eminent defenders of eugenist theories?"

"Eugenics? That theory about improving the human race?"

Holmes nodded. "Francis Galton and his disciples believe that modern society hinders natural selection, allowing 'inferior' individuals to survive and reproduce. They advocate intervention to promote the spread of 'superior' characteristics."

"A controversial theory," I commented.

"And potentially dangerous when pushed to extremes. Imagine a man possessing the technical and financial means to put such ideas into practice on a large scale..."

"You think that Hawthorne..."

Holmes raised a hand to interrupt me. "Let's not jump to hasty conclusions. Let's first gather all the facts."

The rest of the journey passed in thoughtful silence. We arrived in Norwich in the early afternoon and hired a carriage to take us to the small village of Wroxham, on the edge of the Norfolk marshes, where we took a room in the only inn, "The Wild Duck."

The innkeeper, a jovial man with a ruddy face, became animated when Holmes questioned him about the famous airship.

"Oh yes, sir! An extraordinary spectacle, it was! Like a great silver fish in the sky. The whole village came out to see it pass."

"And did you see it disappear?" asked Holmes.

The man shook his head. "No, sir. It continued eastward, toward the marshes. It's Old Tom, the fisherman, who says he saw it last. He claims it suddenly changed direction before disappearing into the fog."

"Could we speak with this Old Tom?"

"You'll probably find him at his dock, near the abandoned mill. He spends his days fishing there, rain or shine."

We set out immediately. The path to the mill crossed damp meadows that gradually gave way to a wilder landscape of marshes and ponds. The air was impregnated with the smell of rotting vegetation and stagnant water. Dark clouds were gathering on the horizon, promising an imminent shower.

We found Old Tom exactly where the innkeeper had indicated, sitting on a dilapidated dock, his fishing line dipping into the murky water. He was a stooped old man, his face weathered by the elements, his hands gnarled like tree roots. His faded blue eyes lit up when Holmes mentioned the airship.

"Ah, that strange flying machine!" he exclaimed, nodding vigorously. "Never seen anything like it in seventy years of living in these marshes, sir."

"Can you tell us exactly what you observed?" asked Holmes.

The old man set down his fishing rod and rubbed his chin thoughtfully.

"It was a misty morning, as we often have around here. I was at my usual spot when I heard a strange humming. Then this thing appeared, majestic as a silver swan. It was flying low, just above the reeds."

"And then?"

"Here's what's curious, sir. It suddenly slowed, as if it was going to stop. Then lights came on under its belly. Red, green, then a very bright white light. After that, it changed course, turning south instead of continuing east as it had been."

"Toward the south?" I intervened. "You're certain?"

"As sure as my name is Thomas Fenton, sir. I know directions like the back of my hand. It went due south, then disappeared into the mist."

Holmes reflected for a moment. "Was there anything unusual in its appearance? Any sign of mechanical trouble?"

The old man shook his head. "No, sir. It seemed perfectly sound. That's why I found it strange that it would change direction like that. As if..."

"As if what?" Holmes encouraged him.

"As if it was responding to a signal," Old Tom finished, lowering his voice. "Those lights under the belly of the craft... they looked like they were responding to something on the ground."

Holmes turned sharply to the old man. "Did you see any other lights in the marshes that day?"

Old Tom hesitated for a moment. "Well... it might have been nothing, but I thought I glimpsed a reflection, like a mirror being waved in the sun, coming from the direction of the old Wroxham tower."

"The old tower?"

"A ruin half swallowed by the marsh, about three miles from here. Used to be a watchtower, they say. Nobody ever goes there, it's too dangerous with the quicksand all around."

Holmes turned to me, a gleam of excitement in his eyes. "Watson, I believe we have found our next destination."

As we took leave of the old fisherman, the first drops of rain began to fall. A spring shower was brewing, and the exploration of the mysterious Wroxham tower promised to be as wet as it was perilous.

The rain intensified as we moved away from Old Tom's dock, quickly transforming the path into a muddy, treacherous surface. Holmes walked with a determined step, his collar turned up against the elements, while I struggled to maintain his pace while avoiding the puddles that were forming before my eyes.

"Holmes, are you certain this expedition is reasonable in such weather?" I asked as a gust of icy wind hit us full on. "These marshes can become dangerous when saturated with water."

"That's precisely why we must hurry, my dear Watson," he replied without slowing down. "If our assumptions are correct, the clues we're seeking could be erased by this rain. Moreover, I greatly prefer facing the elements to wasting precious time."

I sighed, resigned to following my friend into this new perilous adventure. Our progress became more arduous as we ventured deeper into the marshes. The reeds, several feet tall, whipped our faces, and the ground became increasingly spongy underfoot. Several times I had to pull Holmes out of a particularly treacherous bog, and he returned the favor shortly after.

After nearly an hour of this grueling march, we finally caught sight of the tower's silhouette. It was a decrepit structure of gray stone, half collapsed, rising bleakly in the middle of an expanse of stagnant water. It evoked the last vestige of a forgotten world, abandoned to the implacable forces of nature.

"We'll have to cross this expanse of water to reach it," observed Holmes, scanning the surroundings. "And I don't see an obvious passage."

"Old Tom mentioned quicksand," I reminded him with concern.

Holmes crouched to examine the ground at the water's edge. He picked up a long branch and methodically plunged it in different spots.

"Interesting," he murmured. "The bottom seems solid here, but becomes dangerously soft a few feet further. However..." He pointed to a series of stones barely visible at the water's surface. "Do you see these stones, Watson? They seem to form a path."

"Stepping stones? But they appear ancient and probably unstable."

"No doubt, but they constitute our best option." Holmes straightened up. "I'll go first. Follow my steps exactly."

With surprising agility, he launched himself onto the first stone, then the second. I followed cautiously, aware that a misstep could send me into the muddy depths of the marsh. The water was icy, and several times I felt the stones wobble dangerously under my weight.

We finally reached a small island of solid ground on which the ruined tower stood. Its gaping entrance, framed by mossy stones, seemed to invite us into its dark depths.

Holmes took out his magnifying glass and began examining the muddy ground around the tower.

"Look carefully, Watson," he said, pointing to barely perceptible traces. "These footprints have been partially erased by the rain, but one can still discern their shape."

I knelt beside him. "Boots... of substantial size, I'd say."

"Precisely. And notice the depth of the impression on the right side, compared to that of the left."

"The man was limping?"

"Or carrying something heavy on his right shoulder. And look at this." Holmes pointed to a series of parallel marks. "These grooves come from a crate or chest that was dragged to the tower entrance."

We cautiously entered the dilapidated building. The interior was damp and smelled of mold, but surprisingly, the floor seemed to have been recently cleared of debris that must have accumulated there for decades. A spiral staircase, partially collapsed, led up to the upper floor.

"Someone has certainly used this place recently," I murmured.

Holmes nodded silently, his gaze scrutinizing every corner. He approached a wall and passed his hand over the stone. "Fresh soot. A lamp was fixed here."

He continued his methodical inspection and suddenly stopped before an object half buried in the mud. He bent down to pick it up: it was a small piece of shiny metal, about the size of a coin.

"By Jupiter, Watson! Do you know what this is?"

I examined the object. "A fragment of the same alloy used for the airship?"

"Exactly!" His face lit up with that expression I knew so well, the one that announced a breakthrough in the investigation. "And see these markings engraved on the edge... they are partial coordinates."

He carefully slipped the fragment into an envelope which he tucked in his pocket. We continued our exploration, cautiously climbing the unstable steps to the upper floor. Part of the roof had collapsed, letting in the rain and the gray light of day.

Holmes approached an opening in the wall that must once have been a window. From there, one had an unobstructed view of the surrounding marshes.

"The ideal place to send a light signal," he commented. "From here, one could easily attract the attention of an airship passing at low altitude."

"But to what end would they divert their own airship?" I asked, perplexed.

Holmes was about to answer when an ominous cracking sounded beneath our feet. Before we could react, the floor partially gave way. I managed to throw myself backward, but Holmes was less fortunate. He half disappeared into the opening, holding on only by the strength of his arms.

"Holmes!" I cried, rushing to pull him out of the hole.

With effort, we managed to get him back onto the solid part of the floor. He was covered in dust and a scratch was bleeding on his cheek, but he seemed more annoyed than injured.

"Thank you, Watson," he said, dusting off his clothes. "I should have been more careful. This structure is even more unstable than I thought."

Nevertheless, he approached the opening and, lying on his stomach, illuminated the space below with his lantern.

"Well, this is most instructive," he murmured. "Look, Watson."

I approached cautiously and looked into the hole. Below, half buried under the debris, were several objects: a signal lamp, similar to those used in the navy, empty metal boxes that had contained fuel, and what appeared to be a rudimentary wireless telegraph apparatus.

"Good heavens!" I exclaimed. "A signaling station!"

"Exactly. And look at this mark on the lamp." Holmes pointed to an engraved symbol: a simple lightning bolt crossing a circle.

"I don't recognize this symbol."

"It's the emblem of the Promethean League. The fire stolen from the gods." Holmes straightened up, his eyes gleaming with excitement despite our precarious situation. "I believe, Watson, that we have found proof that the airship did not disappear by accident, but was deliberately diverted to a specific destination. And I think I know where."

An even more threatening cracking reminded us of the imminent danger of collapse.

"I suggest we continue this discussion on more stable ground," I said, heading toward the stairs.

We quickly left the tower and recrossed the stepping stones, now even harder to distinguish as the rain had raised the water level. Once back on solid ground, Holmes took out his map and examined it, shielding the paper from the rain with his body.

"If my calculations are correct, and taking into account Old Tom's testimony regarding the direction taken by the airship, we should look toward Dartmoor."

"Dartmoor? But that's at the other end of the country!"

"Indeed. And that's precisely why no one thought to look there." Holmes put away his map. "We must return to London immediately and verify certain information before pursuing in that direction."

The return to the village was as arduous as the outward journey, the rain having transformed the path into a veritable quagmire. We arrived at the inn soaked and exhausted, but Holmes insisted on taking the first available train to London.

"Every hour counts now, Watson," he said as we quickly changed clothes. "I'm convinced that Hawthorne is preparing something imminent."

The night train brought us back to London in the early hours of morning. A thick fog enveloped the capital, reducing visibility to just a few yards. The streets were almost deserted, except for a few early merchants and workers heading to their jobs.

Holmes hailed a cab to take us to Baker Street. "We must first consult some documents in my office," he explained. "Then we'll pay a little visit to Mycroft. He can provide us with more precise information about Hawthorne's properties in Dartmoor."

The cab moved slowly through the fog, the horse's hooves echoing mournfully on the damp cobblestones. I was about to doze off, overcome by the fatigue from our expedition, when Holmes suddenly shook me by the shoulder.

"Watson! We're being followed!"

I sat up, suddenly alert. "Followed? How can you tell in this fog?"

"I've heard the same carriage behind us since we left the station. And now it's accelerating."

Hardly had he spoken these words when our cab was violently struck from behind. Our driver cursed and tried to gain speed, but the narrow streets and the fog made the maneuver perilous.

"Hold on, Watson!" shouted Holmes as a second impact, even more violent, caused our vehicle to tilt dangerously.

The cab turned abruptly into a narrow alley, trying to shake off our pursuer. For a few moments, we thought we had succeeded, but the sound of hooves warned us that we were still being chased.

"We need to get out," Holmes decided. "As soon as we reach a crossing, we'll jump and disperse into the fog."

Our opportunity came when the cab slowed to negotiate a turn. Holmes opened the door and jumped. I followed immediately, landing hard on the cobblestones. We quickly got to our feet and plunged into an adjacent alley, just as the vehicle pursuing us rushed past.

We felt our way through the fog, trying to orient ourselves. Holmes seemed to have a precise idea of our location, guiding us through a maze of narrow passages.

"We're near Covent Garden," he whispered. "If we can reach the main square, we can blend in with the early morning merchants."

The sound of heavy footsteps behind us froze us in place. A massive silhouette took shape in the mist. Even in the dim light, I immediately recognized the characteristic gait and imposing figure of Jonas Crayle. His right hand, gloved in metal, gleamed faintly in the darkness.

"Mr. Holmes," he said in a hoarse voice. "You seem in quite a hurry to get home."

"Mr. Crayle," Holmes calmly replied. "It's a bit early for a stroll, don't you think?"

The man took a step toward us, revealing that he was not alone. Two other figures stood behind him, their faces concealed by scarves.

"Sir Edward doesn't appreciate people nosing into his affairs," Crayle continued. "He has charged me with delivering you a message: cease your investigation immediately, or the consequences will be... regrettable."

I slipped my hand toward the pocket where I kept my revolver, but Holmes restrained me with a subtle gesture.

"A very kind message," he replied with almost supernatural calm. "But I'm afraid I cannot comply. You see, when I accept a case, I make it a principle to see it through to the end."

Crayle's face hardened. "In that case, you leave me no choice."

He signaled to his men, who advanced toward us. In a quick movement, Holmes threw a small object to the ground that exploded in a cloud of acrid smoke. Taking advantage of the confusion, he pulled me into a frantic race through the alleys.

Curses and the noise of pursuers stumbling in the fog reached us, but we continued to run without looking back. Holmes guided us with surprising confidence, turning and doubling back until the sound of footsteps faded into the distance.

Finally, we emerged onto a wider street where a few stalls were beginning to set up for the morning market. Holmes led us to a fish merchant who was unloading his cart.

"Sir," he said, slipping a coin into the astonished man's hand, "might we sit among your crates for a moment?"

The merchant, surprised but satisfied with the generous tip, directed us to the back of his cart. We crouched among the fish crates, their strong odor serving as an unlikely camouflage.

"Holmes," I panted, catching my breath, "how did Crayle know we were back in London?"

"He must have been watching us from the beginning," Holmes replied in a low voice. "Probably alerted by a telegram sent from Norwich. This confirms my suspicions: we're getting close to the truth, and Hawthorne is concerned enough to resort to intimidation."

"What do we do now?"

"We change our strategy." Holmes took a cautious look over the crates. "Instead of returning to Baker Street, where they would certainly be waiting for us, we'll go directly to see Mycroft at the Diogenes Club. From there, we can organize our expedition to Dartmoor."

After a few additional minutes of surveillance, Holmes determined that the coast was clear. We left our malodorous shelter and headed toward Pall Mall, where Mycroft Holmes's private club was located.

The fog was finally beginning to dissipate, revealing a gray but clear sky. The streets were gradually coming to life, offering us the anonymity of the London crowd. Yet I couldn't help glancing nervously over my shoulder, haunted by the image of that metal hand gleaming in the mist.

III

The Diogenes Club, that temple of silence and refuge for the Empire's most influential minds, was immersed in its habitual quietude when we entered. Mycroft Holmes awaited us in a discrete alcove, his imposing figure half-concealed by a cloud of cigar smoke. Seeing us, he set aside his newspaper and motioned for us to join him.

"You seem to have narrowly escaped a delicate situation, Sherlock," he murmured, observing our clothing still spattered with marsh mud. "I've taken the liberty of ordering tea and scones. You appear to need them."

Holmes declined the offer with an impatient gesture. "We have no time to waste on formalities, Mycroft. I need the plans of all Hawthorne's properties in Dartmoor."

Mycroft smiled, amused by his brother's urgency. He pulled a thick folder from his leather satchel. "I anticipated your request. Sir Edward owns an isolated medieval abbey near Princetown, acquired two years ago under the name of a phantom consortium. Reports from local agents mention unusual nighttime movements."

Holmes studied the documents eagerly. "No official investigation?"

"No tangible evidence. And Hawthorne has supporters in Parliament." Mycroft lowered his voice. "But a shepherd reported seeing bluish lights in the abbey's upper windows, as well as an acrid smell of chemicals."

I leaned forward to examine an aerial photograph of the abbey. The edifice, surrounded by desolate moorland, featured a recently reconstructed wing, camouflaged by false ruins. "A disguised hangar?"

"Precisely, Watson!" Holmes pointed to a detail in the image. "See these marks on the ground? Wheel tracks too regular to be natural. An airship requires a vast landing area."

Mycroft nodded. "I've mobilized a discreet army unit. They'll be ready to intervene in twelve hours."

Holmes rose abruptly. "Twelve hours is too long. Hawthorne knows we're on his trail. Watson and I will leave immediately."

The express train to Devon sped through the English countryside, but the idyllic landscape contrasted with the palpable tension in our compartment. Holmes, seated across from me, meticulously cleaned his Webley revolver while outlining his plan.

"The abbey has three entrances according to the plans. You'll take the eastern one with the soldiers, while I'll enter through the underground passages."

I protested. "You're planning to go alone? That's madness!"

He slid a map toward me. "The underground passages are too narrow for a team. But look here..." His finger traced a network of medieval tunnels leading to the abbey's cellars. "A secret entrance here, behind the Black Tor waterfall."

The train stopped at Princetown station under a driving rain. A captain with a gray mustache awaited us, surrounded by six soldiers in civilian clothes.

"Captain Hargreave, at your service, Mr. Holmes. Our men have surrounded the abbey from a distance. No movement since our arrival."

Holmes studied the moor through his binoculars. "The windows of the east wing are camouflaged. See those blue-tinted panes? Protection against prying eyes... and gas leaks."

Night was falling when we reached the Black Tor waterfall. The icy water streamed over a rocky face concealing the entrance to the underground passages. Holmes, dressed in dark clothing, checked his waterproof lamp.

"Stay a hundred paces behind me, Watson. These tunnels are booby-trapped."

The damp darkness engulfed us. Our lamps cut arcs of light on the seeping walls. Holmes moved forward with feline precision, avoiding barely visible wires strung at ankle height.

"Primitive alarms," he murmured. "But connected to what?"

The answer came suddenly in the form of a metallic creak. A rusty blade swept through the space where we had been a second earlier.

"Medieval mechanisms reactivated," Holmes growled, examining the trap. "The perverse ingenuity of a modern mind."

After thirty minutes of breathless progress, a light appeared at the end of the tunnel. Muffled voices reached us, along with a familiar mechanical hum.

The vaulted chamber where the underground passages ended housed the missing airship. The craft, even more imposing than in the plans, gleamed under electric lamps. A team of workers busied themselves loading canisters marked with the Prometheus symbol.

Holmes pulled me behind a pillar. "Look, Watson. The canisters are connected to a spray system under the cockpit."

A burst of voices echoed. Sir Edward Hawthorne himself was descending a metal staircase, Dr. Loxley at his side. The chemist looked pale, her hands bound by discreet handcuffs.

"You've betrayed our noble cause, doctor," Hawthorne thundered. "Fortunately, your formula is perfect. After this final test, nothing will stop humanity's purification."

Loxley proudly raised her chin. "Your gas won't kill only the 'undesirables.' Without my antidote, it will also mutilate your so-called elect!"

This retort was met with a cruel laugh. Jonas Crayle emerged from the shadows, his metal hand clutching a wrench. "The antidote is already synthesized. Your notes were sufficiently detailed."

Holmes whispered to me: "The hangar has four exits. Alert Hargreave: he must cut them all off. I'll go..."

A cracking sound betrayed our presence. Crayle turned his head toward our hiding place, an evil smile on his lips.

"Come out, Holmes!" Crayle roared, brandishing a pistol. "Or I'll blow up the canisters right now!"

We emerged slowly. Hawthorne, initially surprised, quickly regained his arrogance.

"Admirable insight, Mr. Holmes. Too bad you won't be able to appreciate my triumph."

Holmes maintained a troubling calm. "A chemical weapon, Hawthorne? Even for a eugenicist, that's low."

"A necessary purge!" the industrialist flared. "This gas will eliminate the weak, the sick, the misfits. Only the strong will survive."

During this dialogue, I had noticed Dr. Loxley discreetly indicating a switch on the wall. Holmes followed my gaze and nodded imperceptibly.

"Your mistake, Hawthorne," Holmes continued while slowly advancing, "was underestimating your henchmen's loyalty. Do you know what Crayle does with your secret funds?"

The diversion worked. Hawthorne turned toward Crayle, a moment Holmes exploited to lunge for the switch. The room was plunged into darkness.

In the confusion, I heard the metallic click of Crayle's hand, Loxley's cry, then a detonation. When the emergency lamps came on, the scene was apocalyptic:

Holmes had subdued Hawthorne with an arm lock, while Crayle, struck in the temple by Loxley's metal hand (she had turned her handcuffs against her captor), lay unconscious. Hargreave's soldiers were bursting in through all the exits.

Two days later, before a crackling fire, Holmes summarized the case between violin chords.

"Hawthorne planned to release his gas during the opening of Parliament. Crayle was then to impose martial law with imposters under his command. Fortunately, Dr. Loxley had altered the formula."

I raised my glass of brandy. "And her antidote?"

"Distributed to law enforcement as of yesterday. As for the Promethean League, Mycroft is overseeing its... dissolution."

Holmes's violin began a triumphant melody. Outside, the London fog enveloped Baker Street, protective, while another threat to the Empire was extinguished.

THE CHILD OF THE FOG

I

The autumn of 1889 was remarkable for its persistent fog that enveloped London in a grayish shroud day after day. On that late October morning, I remember gazing from our Baker Street window at the ghostly spectacle of passers-by materializing and then vanishing in the opaque mist, like fleeting specters.

My friend Sherlock Holmes was deeply immersed in a meticulous study of The Times, his attention particularly captivated by the classified advertisements, which he sometimes referred to as the "barometer of human troubles." Nearly a week had passed since our last case, and I knew my companion well enough to detect the first signs of that feverish restlessness that seized him when his exceptional mind lacked stimulation.

"Watson," he suddenly said without looking up from his newspaper, "have you noticed the increase in reported disappearances lately? Three in two weeks. That's quite unusual for this season."

I didn't have the opportunity to respond, as we were interrupted by the hasty ringing of our doorbell, followed almost immediately by rapid steps on the stairs and eager knocks at our door.

"Enter!" called Holmes, folding his newspaper.

The door burst open to reveal a man in his thirties, dressed with the elegant sobriety of a prosperous merchant. His blond hair, usually well-ordered judging by the careful part, was disheveled, and his face betrayed deep anguish. His eyes, reddened from lack of sleep, nervously scanned the room with palpable anxiety.

"Mr. Holmes?" he asked, his voice revealing a slight tremor.

"I am he," my friend replied, indicating a chair. "Please, sit down. You have made a long journey this morning, and in a state of considerable agitation."

The man sank into the chair, visibly surprised.

"How can you know I've come from far away?"

Holmes sketched a discreet smile. "The mud on your boots is characteristic of the clay soils of Essex, not the streets of London. As for your anxious state, it can be read in every detail of your person, from your poorly adjusted shirt collar to the nail of your left thumb, visibly bitten in recent hours. But please, tell us about the matter that brings you here."

"My name is Thomas Sunlight," our visitor began, straightening up. "I own a prosperous haberdashery in the Cheapside district. Mr. Holmes, it concerns my son, Edmund... He has disappeared."

His voice broke on these last words.

"I am sorry to hear that," said Holmes with a rare display of compassion. "Please give us all the relevant details. How old is the child?"

"Two and a half years, sir. A lively and joyful little boy..." Sunlight pulled a photograph from his inside pocket and handed it to us. It showed a toddler with blond curls and a mischievous look, sitting on the lap of an elegant woman with delicate features.

"This is Edmund with my wife, Victoria. The photograph was taken barely two months ago."

Holmes examined the image carefully before passing it to me.

"Under what circumstances did your son disappear?"

Sunlight took a deep breath before continuing. "Edmund was staying with his maternal grandparents, Sir Edward and Lady Amelia Farnsworth, at their estate in Lower Thornfield, Essex. It's a small, isolated village. My wife usually spent a few days there each autumn, but this year, she fell ill... A persistent influenza that confined her to bed. We had agreed that Edmund would still go to his grandparents, accompanied by his nurse, Miss Perkins."

"And when exactly did the disappearance occur?" inquired Holmes, his eyes half-closed, in that attitude of concentration I knew so well.

"The day before yesterday, late in the afternoon. Edmund was playing in the enclosed garden of the manor. Miss Perkins left for a few minutes to fetch her coat, as the weather was growing chilly. When she returned, the child was gone."

"Was the garden gate locked?"

"That's the mystery, Mr. Holmes. The gate was closed but not locked. Sir Edward claims that Edmund could have opened it himself and ventured outside. Search parties were organized immediately. The garden opens onto quite a dense forest..."

Holmes leaped to his feet and began pacing the room.

"Has the local police been notified?"

"Of course," replied Sunlight with a disdainful grimace. "Inspector Forrester is leading the investigation, but he seems convinced that it's either an accident-the child got lost in the woods-or..." He hesitated, as if the idea was unbearable to him. "Or that a wild animal carried him off."

"Have any witnesses spotted the child after his disappearance from the garden?"

"Two people claim to have seen him. A young blacksmith's apprentice says he glimpsed Edmund walking alone on the path leading to the forest. An old gardener corroborates this testimony. But Mr. Holmes..." Sunlight leaned forward, lowering his voice. "I don't believe the accident theory."

"Why is that?" asked Holmes, stopping abruptly.

"The Farnsworths never approved of my marriage to their daughter. I'm just a shopkeeper, you see, while they belong to an old aristocratic family... impoverished, certainly, but proud of their rank. Since Edmund's birth, they have repeatedly attempted to influence his upbringing, to distance him from me..."

"Are you suggesting that the grandparents might be involved in the disappearance of their own grandson?" I interjected, astonished.

"I don't know what to think, doctor," replied Sunlight, turning to me. "But I know my son. He's a cautious child who would never have opened that gate by himself to venture into the unknown."

Holmes resumed his seat in his armchair, joining his long fingers under his chin in that meditative posture that was familiar to him.

"Mr. Sunlight, I will take your case. Dr. Watson and I will take the next train to Essex. Meanwhile, return to your wife and provide us with a letter of introduction to the Farnsworths."

Our visitor's face lit up with new hope. "Thank you, Mr. Holmes. A thousand times, thank you."

"One last question," added Holmes as Sunlight rose. "Do you have enemies, in your professional or personal life, who might wish to harm you through your son?"

Sunlight seemed to reflect for a moment. "No, Mr. Holmes. My business prospers without provoking any particular jealousies. As for my private life, it is exemplary in its ordinariness."

After his departure, Holmes remained silent, mechanically puffing on the pipe he had just lit. I knew this concentrated expression too well to interrupt him.

"What do you think, Holmes?" I finally ventured.

"I think, my dear Watson," he replied, turning to me, "that you would do well to prepare your suitcase. This case presents several intriguing aspects. Did you notice the peculiar wear on Mr. Sunlight's gloves?"

"His gloves?" I repeated, perplexed. "I observed nothing particular."

Holmes smiled with that indulgence tinged with amusement that he often reserved for me.

"Exactly, Watson. Nothing particular for a merchant who handles fabrics daily. However, I noted three other details that merit our attention. But come, we'll discuss them on the train. If we hurry, we can catch the eleven o'clock train to Chelmsford."

As I gathered a few belongings and my trusty revolver, I couldn't help thinking of that little boy lost in the autumn fog. The image of his smiling face in the photograph contrasted cruelly with the paternal anguish we had witnessed. Little did I know then that this case would lead us into the darkest corners of the human soul, where the unspeakable secrets of respectable families lie hidden.

The train to Chelmsford wound through the English countryside, offering through its fogged windows the melancholy spectacle of an autumnal landscape. The woods in ochre and vermilion hues appeared and disappeared in the mist like fleeting visions, while the valleys and fields followed one another in a hypnotic monotony. Holmes observed this scene with an abstracted eye, his mind evidently occupied with reflections far removed from these bucolic considerations.

Thomas Sunlight had joined us at Liverpool Street Station, giving us a letter of introduction to the Farnsworths as well as some personal belongings of the missing child, which Holmes had carefully examined before storing them in his valise. To my great surprise, my friend had insisted that the father accompany us.

"Tell me more about Sir Edward and Lady Amelia Farnsworth," Holmes asked our travel companion, breaking a long silence.

Sunlight, who was contemplating the landscape with an absent air, turned toward us. "Sir Edward comes from a lineage dating back to the Wars of the Roses. The Farnsworths once owned several properties in the county, but successive generations have gradually squandered this fortune. The Lower Thornfield manor is their last possession, and even it is largely mortgaged, according to what Victoria has confided to me."

"A declining aristocracy, then," commented Holmes, drawing on his pipe. "And Lady Amelia?"

"The youngest daughter of the Earl of Westmoreland. A marriage that was considered a misalliance by her family, although the Farnsworths still had their prestige at the time. She is a woman..." He searched for words. "A cold woman, Mr. Holmes. In ten years of marriage to their daughter, I have never managed to win her sympathy."

"And Victoria, your wife, how does she accommodate this situation?"

"Victoria is a remarkable woman," replied Sunlight, his face softening at the mention of his wife. "She was raised in the cult of rank and propriety, but she chose to break free from these prejudices by marrying me. We have built our happiness together, far from the rigors of her upbringing."

"You mentioned that she is currently suffering from influenza. Is this usual? Is her health generally fragile?"

A shadow crossed Sunlight's face. "No, Victoria usually enjoys excellent health. This flu struck her suddenly, three days before Edmund's visit to his grandparents. She insisted on postponing, but I suggested that the country air would be good for our son." He clenched his fists. "If only I had heeded her reluctance..."

"Was the child accompanied only by his nurse?" Holmes continued, imperturbable.

"Yes, Miss Perkins. A woman in her forties, absolutely devoted to Edmund. She has been devastated since his disappearance, constantly blaming herself for leaving the garden for a few minutes."

Holmes nodded thoughtfully. "And you, Mr. Sunlight, tell me about your business. You mentioned having no enemies, but perhaps you have competitors? Recent transactions that might have provoked resentment?"

"My haberdashery is not a considerable business, although it is prosperous," replied Sunlight. "I recently acquired an adjacent property to expand, but the transaction proceeded without a hitch. As for my competitors, our relations are cordial, even friendly with some."

"No inheritances at stake? No insurance policies on the child?"

For the first time, Sunlight appeared slightly offended. "I don't see the connection with my son's disappearance, Mr. Holmes. But to answer your question, Edmund has no particular inheritance. As for insurance..." He hesitated. "I did indeed take out a policy for Edmund three months ago, as I did for my wife and myself. A simple precautionary measure that my notary advised."

Holmes exchanged with me a look that I could not interpret, then abruptly changed the subject.

"Do the grandparents have other grandchildren?"

"No, Victoria is their only child. Edmund is therefore the sole heir to the name, although he bears mine. Sir Edward has reproached me more than once that the Farnsworth name would die with him."

The conversation was interrupted by our arrival at Chelmsford station. We descended onto the platform swept by a damp wind, where a connection awaited us for the final portion of our journey to Lower Thornfield.

The small local train that took us there was almost empty, except for a drowsy clergyman and a mature lady accompanied by her servant. When we finally reached the tiny Lower Thornfield station, the day was already declining, drowning the landscape in a twilight light that reinforced the oppressive atmosphere of the place.

On the deserted platform stood a massive man in his fifties, whose ruddy face and salt-and-pepper side-whiskers framed an expression of frank perplexity. He approached as soon as he saw us.

"Mr. Sunlight," he greeted with a nod, before turning to us. "And you must be Mr. Holmes. I am Inspector Forrester. Sir Edward informed me of your arrival."

His tone revealed a mixture of reluctance and curiosity. Holmes shook his hand with that distant courtesy he reserved for provincial law enforcement representatives.

"Inspector Forrester, I hope our collaboration will be fruitful. Do you have any news regarding young Edmund's disappearance?"

The inspector shook his head. "We've combed the forest for two miles around. Not the slightest trace of the little one. I'm afraid we're facing a tragic accident, perhaps involving a predator. We've reported the presence of a fox in the area these past few weeks."

I saw Sunlight pale at this mention, but Holmes dismissed this theory with an impatient wave of his hand.

"A fox does not attack a child of this age, Inspector, unless the animal is rabid, in which case its erratic behavior would have been noticed well before. Have you questioned all potential witnesses?"

"Of course," replied Forrester, visibly piqued. "The entire village has been questioned. Only young Simmons and old Hodge saw the child outside the garden. Their testimonies match perfectly."

"Sometimes, a too-perfect match is more suspicious than a slight divergence," Holmes murmured, more to himself than to his interlocutor. "Could you take us to the Farnsworth manor?"

A cab was waiting near the station. During the journey, I observed through the window the village of Lower Thornfield revealing itself in the growing dusk. Thirty houses at most, clustered around a square where stood a small Norman church and what appeared to be a tavern. The few passersby followed us with their eyes with that suspicious curiosity characteristic of small rural communities toward strangers.

"The village has hardly changed in two centuries," commented the inspector, following my gaze. "The same families have lived here for generations. The Farnsworths are considered the lords of the place, although their influence has considerably diminished."

"Did the villagers actively participate in the search?" Holmes inquired.

"Eagerly," confirmed Forrester. "Everyone knew little Edmund by sight. His visits were noted events here."

We soon left the village to take an avenue lined with century-old elms, whose bare branches formed a sinister vault above our heads. Around a bend finally appeared the Farnsworth manor, an imposing mass of gray stone whose numerous chimneys stood out against the darkening sky. Some windows were lit, casting rectangles of yellow light on the neglected lawn.

As we approached, I was struck by the both majestic and dilapidated aspect of the residence. The building evidently dated from the Tudor period, with Victorian additions that unsuccessfully attempted to mask the wear of time. An entire wing seemed abandoned, its windows boarded up.

The cab stopped before a columned portico. The door opened before we even had time to descend, revealing the slender silhouette of a man about sixty years old, with a stately bearing and piercing gaze. His gray hair was impeccably combed, and his attire, although slightly worn, betrayed an elegance from another time.

"Sir Edward Farnsworth, I presume," said Holmes, stepping forward.

The man looked us over with undisguised coldness.

"Mr. Holmes. Thomas has informed me of your arrival. I don't see how a private detective can be more effective than the local law enforcement, but if it can reassure Edmund's parents... Do come in, night is falling and the fog is thickening."

With these less than welcoming words, he stepped aside to let us enter the ancestral home of the Farnsworths, where awaited us, though we did not yet know it, the first clues of this troubling affair that I would later record in my annals under the title of "The Mystery of the Child of the Fog."

II

The entrance hall of the Farnsworth manor presented a striking spectacle of faded grandeur. A majestic staircase rose to the upper floor, its finely carved balusters testifying to a bygone era of splendor. Austere ancestral portraits, their gilded frames having lost their luster, observed us with frozen disapproval from the paneled walls. An imposing chandelier, with several candles missing, dispensed a flickering light that accentuated the shadows rather than dispelling them.

Sir Edward led us through this melancholy setting to an impressively proportioned drawing room. A fire roared in a monumental fireplace, the only source of warmth in this room where dampness seemed to have taken up residence for generations. The furniture, though elegant, bore the stigmata of insufficient maintenance, and the heavy drapes framing the windows were worn in places. Standing near the fireplace was a tall, thin woman with an emaciated face dominated by ice-blue eyes. Her gray hair was pulled into a severe bun that accentuated the rigidity of her features. Her black dress, impeccably cut but outdated in style, reinforced the general impression of a person anchored in a past she refused to abandon.

"Lady Amelia," Sir Edward introduced without warmth, "this is Mr. Sherlock Holmes and his assistant, Dr. Watson. Thomas has engaged them to investigate Edmund's disappearance."

Lady Amelia inclined her head slightly in greeting, her gaze assessing us with calculated coldness.

"Gentlemen," she said in a remarkably clear voice for a woman of her age. "Your reputation precedes you, Mr. Holmes. I sincerely hope your talents can help us find our grandson."

Although her words were courteous, I couldn't help but notice the absence of genuine emotion in her voice. Holmes, whose piercing gaze had been scanning the room since our entrance, bowed slightly.

"Lady Amelia, Sir Edward, please accept my condolences for this ordeal. If you would permit me, I'd like to ask you some questions about the exact circumstances of the disappearance."

At a gesture from Sir Edward, we took seats in armchairs with sagging cushions. Inspector Forrester settled in a corner of the room, as if wishing to be forgotten, while Thomas Sunlight remained standing, visibly uncomfortable in these surroundings.

"I assume the inspector has already questioned you in detail," Holmes began, "but I would appreciate hearing your personal account of the events. At what exact time did you last see Edmund?"

Sir Edward and his wife exchanged a brief glance before the former spoke.

"It was approximately four o'clock in the afternoon. Edmund was playing in the enclosed garden, under Miss Perkins's supervision. I saw him from my office window as he was playing near the basin with a little boat I had made for him."

"And you, Lady Amelia?" Holmes inquired.

"I wasn't at home at that moment," she replied with slight hesitation. "I had gone to visit Mrs. Pemberton, an ailing friend in the village. I returned around five o'clock to learn the terrible news."

"Miss Perkins claims she was absent for a few minutes to fetch warm clothing for the child," Sunlight intervened with a hint of bitterness. "How could she leave him alone, knowing the garden opens onto the forest?"

"The garden is perfectly enclosed, Thomas," replied Sir Edward with irritation. "Miss Perkins couldn't have anticipated that the boy would manage to open the gate. Besides, if Victoria had been present, as was initially planned, perhaps-"

"I forbid you to implicate my wife in this tragedy!" exclaimed Sunlight, his face flushed.

Holmes raised a pacifying hand. "Gentlemen, please. Our emotions, though understandable, won't help us find the child." Turning to Sir Edward, he continued: "This gate, was it usually locked?"

"Always," affirmed Sir Edward. "Miss Perkins swears she closed it that morning. We don't know how Edmund could have opened it."

"May I see Miss Perkins?" asked Holmes.

"She is bedridden, under sedatives," Lady Amelia intervened. "The doctor has prescribed complete rest. The poor woman has been in a state of extreme prostration since the incident."

Holmes nodded, his face remaining inscrutable. "I would like to examine Edmund's room, if you have no objection, then the garden where he was last seen."

"By all means," conceded Sir Edward with a weary wave of his hand. "Thomas will show you the way, he knows the house."

As we rose, Holmes posed one final question that seemed to catch our hosts off guard.

"Did Edmund have a habit of venturing out alone without supervision? Was he naturally reckless or, on the contrary, cautious?"

A silence settled, as if everyone hesitated to answer. Finally, it was Lady Amelia who spoke.

"Edmund is an intelligent and curious child, but by no means reckless. He has always shown... reluctance to stray from adults he knows."

"That's precisely why I find it inconceivable that he would have opened that gate on his own," added Sunlight.

Holmes made no comment, but I noticed that particular gleam in his eye that always signaled when a significant detail had caught his attention.

Thomas Sunlight led us upstairs via the grand staircase. The steps groaned under our footsteps, betraying the venerable age of the building. The hallway we emerged into was dimly lit by a few wall sconces, some of which appeared not to have been lit for some time, judging by the thick layer of dust covering them.

"The east wing is practically abandoned," explained Sunlight, following my gaze. "The

Farnsworths now occupy only the west wing and the central part of the manor. The upkeep of such a property is far beyond their current means."

We arrived at a door painted in pale blue, adorned with a small wooden sign engraved with the name "Edmund." The room that greeted our view contrasted singularly with the rest of the dwelling in its cheerfulness and maintenance. The walls were papered with maritime scenes, and a brightly colored carpet covered the floor. A crib occupied one corner of the room, while a matching oak wardrobe and dresser completed the furnishings. On a low table were carefully arranged toys: lead soldiers, small wooden animals, and a miniature train.

Holmes methodically examined the room, dwelling on each detail with the intense concentration so characteristic of him. He opened the dresser drawers, inspected the wardrobe's contents, and even knelt to examine underneath the bed. I saw him collect some fibers from the carpet, which he carefully placed in an envelope.

"Have the clothes Edmund was wearing on the day of his disappearance been identified?" he asked Sunlight.

"Yes. Blue overalls, a white shirt, a beige wool vest, and brown boots. I brought a recent photograph where he is wearing this outfit."

Holmes studied the image then tucked it into his pocket. "Now show me the garden, please."

We went back downstairs and traversed part of the ground floor to a glass door that opened onto the back of the property. Twilight had given way to night, but someone had had the foresight to light lanterns that marked the main paths of the garden. Despite the darkness, I could discern a carefully arranged space, with geometric flowerbeds and trimmed hedges. In the center was a circular basin where the little boat mentioned by Sir Edward still floated.

Holmes immediately approached the famous gate, located at the far end of the garden. It was a wrought-iron structure about four feet high, integrated into a stone wall that delimited the property. Beyond it, one could make out the dark mass of the forest.

Kneeling near the gate, Holmes took out his magnifying glass and minutely examined the latch mechanism. I saw him scrape a substance from the metal, which he placed in another of his envelopes. Then he turned his attention to the ground, both inside and outside the garden.

"Watson," he suddenly said, "lend me your match."

I complied, and by the light of the flame, Holmes carefully scrutinized a series of barely visible footprints in the loose earth near the gate. His face animated with an expression I knew well – one that announced a significant discovery.

"Interesting," he murmured to himself.

"What have you found?" asked Sunlight, who had joined us.

"Several things, but nothing conclusive for now," Holmes evasively replied. He straightened up and examined the path leading into the woods. "Is this where the witnesses claim to have seen Edmund walking away?"

"Yes," confirmed Sunlight. "First Jack Simmons, the blacksmith's apprentice, then William Hodge, the gardener, a bit further down the path."

Holmes followed the path for about twenty yards, stopping frequently to examine the ground by the light of his lantern. Darkness was now complete, and fog was insinuating itself between the trees, creating a ghostly atmosphere around us.

As we returned toward the manor, we crossed paths with an elderly man pushing a wheelbarrow filled with gardening tools. Despite his advanced age, he stood remarkably upright, and his weather-beaten face displayed an expression of quiet dignity.

"Ah, Hodge," Sunlight called out. "This is Mr. Sherlock Holmes and Dr. Watson. They're investigating Edmund's disappearance."

The old man respectfully touched his cap. "Gentlemen."

"Mr. Hodge," said Holmes with unusual courtesy, "I would like to speak with you tomorrow about what you saw. For now, could you tell me if you noticed anything unusual in the days preceding young Edmund's disappearance?"

Hodge seemed to reflect, his eyes faded by age peering into the distance. "Nothing out of the ordinary, sir. Except perhaps..."

"Yes?" Holmes encouraged him.

"Well, I spotted a figure prowling near the edge of the woods the day before yesterday. Probably a poacher, we get them sometimes in these parts. I didn't pay much attention at the time."

Holmes nodded. "Thank you, Mr. Hodge. We'll discuss all this further tomorrow."

The gardener went on his way, and we returned to the manor. In the hall, we found Inspector Forrester conversing in hushed tones with Sir Edward.

"Have you made any useful discoveries, Mr. Holmes?" asked the inspector with a hint of condescension.

"Some preliminary observations, nothing more," replied my friend with feigned modesty that I knew well. "Inspector, I would like to examine tomorrow the written testimonies you've collected."

"Of course," Forrester reluctantly conceded. "I'll have them sent to your hotel."

"Our hotel?" I repeated, surprised.

"You'll be staying at the Fox & Crown, the village's only inn," Sir Edward intervened. "I've taken the liberty of reserving rooms for you there. Thomas will stay here, naturally."

Holmes nodded. "That's perfect. We'll return tomorrow morning to continue our investigations. Lady Amelia, Sir Edward, thank you for your cooperation."

As we took our leave, I noticed that Holmes cast a final scrutinizing glance at Sir Edward's shoes, neatly aligned near the front door, then at those of the gardener Hodge, muddy and worn, drying on a straw mat.

The journey to the village took place in an oppressive silence. The fog had thickened, transforming familiar contours of the landscape into ghostly and threatening shapes. It was only once we were settled in the nearly deserted common room of the Fox & Crown, before two glasses of steaming whisky, that Holmes finally consented to share his first impressions.

"Well, Watson, what do you think of this case?" he asked me, his gray eyes shining with a gleam I knew well.

"I find the atmosphere of this manor particularly oppressive," I replied honestly. "As for the Farnsworths, they don't seem to display the degree of concern one would expect from grandparents whose grandson has disappeared."

"Excellent observation," approved Holmes. "And did you notice anything else?"

I reflected for a moment. "Lady Amelia claimed to have returned at five o'clock, after learning the news. Yet, if the child disappeared around four o'clock, how could she have been informed of it in the village, unless someone came expressly to notify her?"

Holmes smiled with satisfaction. "Precisely, Watson! Your powers of observation are refining with the years. For my part, I've noted several troubling details. First, the footprints near the gate tell a very different story from the one presented to us. Second, I observed traces on gardener Hodge's shoes that correspond to a type of soil not found in the Farnsworths' garden. And third..." He broke off, observing the entrance to the inn.

I turned to see a robust young man with red hair and a face covered with freckles who had just entered the establishment. His gaze met ours, and he hastily looked away before heading to the counter.

"Our young friend over there," murmured Holmes, "is probably Jack Simmons, the blacksmith's apprentice and one of our key witnesses. Note the state of his sleeves and the recent abrasion on his right hand. Tomorrow, Watson, we'll begin to untangle the web of lies surrounding little Edmund's disappearance. For I am now convinced of one thing: we have been lied to, and quite skillfully."

With these enigmatic words, Holmes emptied his glass and rose, signaling that our conversation was over for the evening. As I followed him toward the stairs leading to our rooms, I couldn't help thinking of the little boy lost in the night and fog, if indeed he was there at all.

The next morning, a timid ray of sunshine pierced the fog as we left the inn to visit the village forge. Holmes had insisted on beginning our day by interrogating Jack Simmons, the blacksmith's apprentice who claimed to have spotted Edmund wandering alone near the forest.

Lower Thornfield was awakening lazily. A few villagers were already going about their business, eyeing us with undisguised curiosity. Our presence seemed to be the subject of all conversations, judging by the whispers that accompanied us as we passed.

The forge stood at the edge of the village, a robust building of stone blackened by decades of smoke. As we approached, the characteristic sound of hammer striking anvil reached us, rhythmic and powerful. In the frame of the wide open door, we distinguished two silhouettes:

one massive and imposing, that of the blacksmith no doubt, and the other thinner, which must have belonged to his apprentice.

"Good morning, gentlemen," Holmes called out as he entered the smoky workshop. "Allow me to introduce myself, Sherlock Holmes, and this is my colleague, Dr. Watson. We're investigating the disappearance of young Edmund Sunlight."

The blacksmith, a colossus with a graying beard and arms as muscular as tree trunks, stared at us for a moment before nodding gravely.

"Peter Blacksmith, sir," he introduced himself, wiping his callused hand on his leather apron before shaking ours. "And this is my apprentice, Jack."

The young man we had seen at the inn the previous evening greeted us with a hesitant nod. Up close, he appeared even younger, perhaps sixteen or seventeen at most. His juvenile features were tense, and his evasive gaze immediately confirmed my suspicions: this boy was hiding something.

"Jack," said Holmes in a surprisingly gentle voice, "I'd like you to tell me exactly what you saw on the afternoon of Edmund's disappearance. Take your time, every detail may be important."

Blacksmith gave an encouraging pat on his apprentice's shoulder. "Go on, lad. Tell these gentlemen what you told me."

Jack nervously wiped his hands on his pants before beginning.

"It was Tuesday afternoon, around quarter past four, I'd say. I was coming back from the Pembertons, where I had delivered horseshoes for their mare. I was taking the shortcut that runs along the wall of the Farnsworth estate when I spotted the little one."

"At what exact distance?" Holmes interrupted.

"About twenty yards, maybe. He was on the path leading to the forest, just past the garden gate."

"And what was he doing?"

"He was walking calmly, as if he were out for a stroll. He looked... curious, I'd say. Not frightened, nor lost. Just a little fellow exploring."

"Was he carrying anything? A toy, perhaps?"

Jack frowned, seeming to make an effort to remember. "I don't think so... Oh, wait! He was holding a small shiny object in his hand. Maybe a spoon or something metallic. I couldn't see clearly."

"Did you call to him? Did you try to approach him?"

The young man suddenly appeared uncomfortable. "No, sir. I didn't think... I mean, it's not uncommon for the little one to play outside when he's at his grandparents'. I assumed someone was watching him."

"From the forest?" asked Holmes, raising a skeptical eyebrow.

"I didn't think it through, sir," replied Jack, his cheeks coloring slightly. "I was in a hurry to get back to the forge. The master was waiting for me for an urgent order."

"Indeed," confirmed Blacksmith. "A repair for the stagecoach. Work that couldn't wait."

Holmes carefully examined Jack's right hand, where the abrasion we had noticed the day before was clearly visible.

"A nasty wound," he commented. "How did you get it?"

"Working with metal, sir," the apprentice replied hastily. "It happens often in our trade."

"Certainly," Holmes conceded. "Tell me, Jack, do you know the Farnsworth family well?"

"Like everyone in the village, sir. They're respectable people."

"And Lady Amelia? Have you had any particular interactions with her?"

I saw the young man imperceptibly stiffen. "No, sir. Why would I have...? She comes to the forge sometimes for the horses, but it's the master who deals with that, not me."

Holmes smiled slightly. "Just curious. One last question: after seeing the child, which route did you take back to the village?"

"The main road, of course."

"And you didn't pass anyone else?"

Jack hesitated for a fraction of a second. "Old Hodge, a bit further on. I actually mentioned to him that I'd seen the little one."

Holmes nodded, then turned to the blacksmith. "Mr. Blacksmith, at what exact time did your apprentice return to the forge that day?"

"Around half past four, I'd say. I was busy with the stagecoach, I didn't pay particular attention."

After a few additional questions that yielded nothing new, we took our leave. Barely had we left the forge when Holmes slowed his pace, allowing Jack and his master to be out of earshot.

"What do you think, Watson?"

"That boy is lying," I stated without hesitation. "But I couldn't say precisely on which point."

"On several points, actually," Holmes confirmed. "Did you notice the state of his shoes?"

I shook my head, confused. "I must admit I did not."

"Traces of red mud. Now, this type of soil is found in only one place in the vicinity: near the stream that flows behind the Farnsworth manor, in the opposite direction from the path he claims to have taken. As for his injury, it was certainly not caused by metal. I can clearly distinguish splinters, probably from wood. And finally, his nervousness increased considerably when I mentioned Lady Amelia."

"Do you think there's a connection between them?"

"It's a hypothesis we must explore. But first, let's visit our second witness, the gardener Hodge."

We found the old man in the vicarage's vegetable garden, methodically trimming a hedge of yew trees. Despite his advanced age, his movements were precise and assured, testifying to a lifetime devoted to this profession.

"Mr. Hodge," Holmes called out, "could you spare us a few minutes?"

The gardener straightened slowly, placing a hand on his aching back, then greeted us with an old-fashioned politeness. "Gentlemen, I am at your disposal."

"I understand you've worked for the Farnsworth family for many years," Holmes began.

"Fifty-three years of good and loyal service, sir," Hodge confirmed with evident pride. "I started as a garden boy under Sir George, the father of the current baronet. I saw the estate in its days of glory, before the difficulties..." He broke off, as if regretting having said too much.

"Sir Edward mentioned financial setbacks," Holmes observed with a confidential tone. "A difficult situation for a family of their standing."

"Times change, sir," the old man sighed. "But it's not for me to comment on my masters' affairs."

"Of course. Let's talk instead about what you saw last Tuesday. Jack Simmons claims he crossed paths with you and mentioned having spotted young Edmund."

Hodge nodded. "That's correct. The boy told me he had seen the little one heading toward the woods. I then hastened in that direction, and I did indeed glimpse the child about a hundred yards away, still on the path."

"Did you try to intercept him?"

"Certainly!" exclaimed the gardener, as if offended by the question. "But at my age, my legs don't carry me as fast as they once did. I called out, but the child didn't hear me - or didn't pay attention. By the time I reached the edge of the woods, he had disappeared. I then turned back to raise the alarm at the manor."

Holmes carefully observed the old man as he spoke, his gaze lingering on his gnarled hands and his worn but immaculately clean clothes.

"Mr. Hodge, how long have you known Jack Simmons?"

The question seemed to surprise the gardener. "Young Jack? Well, since his birth, like all the village children. His father worked in the Farnsworth stables before dying of tuberculosis a few years ago."

"And what sort of boy is he?"

"A good lad, hardworking. A bit hotheaded sometimes, like all young mcn his age, but fundamentally honest."

Holmes nodded pensively. "One last question: did you notice anything unusual regarding Sir Edward or Lady Amelia's behavior before Edmund's disappearance?"

The old gardener suddenly appeared uncomfortable. "I don't see what you mean, sir."

"Unusual visitors, perhaps? Tense conversations? Changes in their habits?"

"I'm just a simple gardener, Mr. Holmes. I tend to plants, not to my masters' affairs."

But his evasive look and the slight trembling of his hands betrayed a new nervousness. Holmes didn't insist, sensing that we would get nothing more for now.

As we were taking our leave, my friend suddenly stopped and turned around. "Oh, just a formality, Mr. Hodge: where exactly were you when Jack Simmons crossed paths with you?"

"On the main road, of course, returning from the village where I had bought seeds."

"And yet," Holmes remarked in an almost detached tone, "the mud on your shoes last night came from the stream bank, to the west of the property. A curious detour for someone returning from the village, which lies to the east."

The old man's face fell. "I... I must have gone there later in the day. With all the commotion, you understand, my memory isn't what it used to be."

Holmes added nothing, but as we walked away, I heard him murmur: "Two witnesses, Watson, and two fragile testimonies. This is becoming most interesting."

We spent the rest of the morning exploring the village, Holmes discreetly asking the inhabitants about the Farnsworths, their financial situation, and their relationships with the rest of the community. At noon, we returned to the Fox & Crown inn for lunch.

The establishment was more animated than the previous evening. Several tables were occupied by nearby farmers who had come for the weekly market, and the hubbub of conversations momentarily ceased at our entrance before resuming with greater vigor, probably enriched with comments about our presence.

We had just finished our meal when Inspector Forrester appeared, a file under his arm.

"Mr. Holmes," he greeted us, taking a seat at our table without being invited. "I've brought the depositions you requested."

"Most kind of you," replied Holmes, quickly scanning the documents. "Is there any news regarding the search?"

Forrester shook his head. "Nothing, unfortunately. I had the stream dragged this morning, without result." He lowered his voice. "Between us, I greatly fear we may never find the child. This forest is vast and full of dangers. A little boy of that age, alone on a cold evening..."

I saw a flash of irritation cross Holmes's gaze, but he merely nodded thoughtfully.

"Inspector, what about the Farnsworth family's background? Have there been any notable incidents in recent years?"

Forrester appeared surprised by the question. "The Farnsworths are above suspicion, Mr. Holmes. Certainly, their fortune has declined, but their reputation remains irreproachable."

"And their relationship with the Pembertons, whom I've heard mentioned?"

The inspector scowled. "An old story. James Pemberton and Sir Edward were once partners in a mining venture that went badly. Sir Edward accuses Pemberton of having ruined him through imprudent investments. Pemberton claims that Sir Edward misappropriated funds. The two families haven't spoken for twenty years."

"Do the Pembertons still live in the village?"

"Old James died last year. His widow and son still occupy the manor at the other end of the village. But I don't see how this could be related to the little one's disappearance."

Holmes didn't respond directly, merely thanking the inspector for the documents. After the latter's departure, my friend remained plunged in silent meditation for several minutes.

"Watson," he finally said, "I'm going to need your assistance this evening for a little experiment. But first, let's return to the Farnsworth manor. I wish to question Miss Perkins, the nurse, if she's in a condition to receive us."

As we left the inn, Holmes explained his plan. He would return alone to the Fox & Crown in the evening, disguised as a traveling merchant, to gather local rumors in the relaxed atmosphere that generally develops after a few pints of beer.

"The villagers will be more inclined to open up to an anonymous traveler than to the famous Sherlock Holmes," he explained. "As for you, my dear friend, I'll ask you to keep an eye on the Farnsworth manor from the edge of the woods. I suspect that some of our actors might arrange to meet there tonight."

As we made our way to the Farnsworth estate, I couldn't help noticing that Holmes seemed unusually preoccupied.

"Is there something particularly troubling you about this case, Holmes?" I inquired.

"What troubles me, Watson," he replied, lowering his voice although we were alone on the path, "is that two witnesses claim to have seen a child who, in all probability, was not where they claim to have seen him."

"What do you mean?"

"The footprints near the gate, Watson. They tell a very different story from the one presented to us. But patience, my friend. Before the end of this day, I think we will have made a considerable step toward the truth."

His enigmatic words left me perplexed, but experience had taught me that Holmes only revealed his deductions at the moment he deemed appropriate. I therefore resigned myself to waiting, while wondering about the nature of the secrets harbored by the Farnsworth manor, and about the fate of the little boy whose absence now haunted this apparently peaceful village.

III

The Farnsworth manor appeared even more sinister beneath the pale light of early afternoon. Clouds had gathered, promising another shower, and the wind stirred the bare branches of the century-old trees that lined the main avenue.

Our visit was brief and unfruitful. Miss Perkins, the nurse, was still bedridden and, according to Lady Amelia, unable to receive anyone. Sir Edward was absent, having gone to Chelmsford on business. As for Thomas Sunlight, he had returned to London to be with his wife, at the insistence of Inspector Forrester who had assured him he would be notified immediately of any developments.

Holmes skillfully concealed his displeasure, but I knew him well enough to perceive his irritation. As we were taking our leave, he stopped abruptly before a small writing desk in the entrance hall.

"A lovely specimen of Georgian marquetry," he commented casually. "Is it a family heirloom, Lady Amelia?"

"Indeed," she replied with a hint of pride. "It belonged to my grandmother."

Holmes examined it more closely, lingering over the finely crafted drawers. "These small drawers are perfect for keeping private correspondence, aren't they?"

I saw a flash of concern cross our hostess's gaze. "I suppose so. But I hardly use this piece of furniture nowadays."

"A pity," Holmes replied, straightening. "Such artisanal objects deserve to maintain their usefulness. Well, we won't trouble you any further. Come, Watson."

Once outside, Holmes quickly led me toward the path leading to the forest. "Our visit wasn't entirely useless," he murmured with an enigmatic smile.

"What did you discover?" I asked, intrigued.

"Did you notice the fine dust on the edge of the writing desk? It was disturbed by recent fingerprints. This piece of furniture is used regularly, contrary to what Lady Amelia claims. Moreover, I glimpsed the corner of an envelope bearing the Bristol postmark slightly protruding from one of the drawers."

"Bristol?"

"Indeed, Watson. But let's save that for later. For now, let's focus on what the forest has to reveal."

We had reached the edge of the woods. The forest path was barely visible, overrun with vegetation and muddy from recent rains. Holmes stopped, scrutinizing the ground carefully.

"Look, Watson. What do you see?"

I knelt to examine the spot he indicated. "Footprints, I believe. But they're almost erased by the rain."

"Almost, but not entirely. Observe their size and arrangement."

I squinted. "They're too large to belong to a child. And they... they go in both directions. Someone came and then went back."

"Excellent deduction," Holmes approved. "These prints date from the afternoon of the disappearance, before the evening rain. They belong to a man of medium height, wearing dress shoes-note the characteristic shape of the heel. Let's continue."

We ventured into the forest, Holmes progressing slowly, stopping frequently to examine the ground and surrounding vegetation. After about a hundred yards, he halted near a bramble thicket.

"Ah," he murmured, kneeling cautiously. With his nimble fingers, he extracted a small fragment of blue fabric caught on the thorns. "Blue cotton twill. The same material as Edmund's overalls."

My heart sank. "Holmes, does this mean the child actually passed through here?"

"Certainly someone wearing a similar garment," he replied evasively. He placed the fabric in one of his envelopes and continued his exploration.

Twenty yards further, he discovered a second clue: a mother-of-pearl button half-buried in the mud. "A child's shirt button," he commented, examining it with his magnifying glass. "But observe carefully, Watson. What do you notice?"

I leaned over the object. "It seems... clean. Almost new."

"Exactly! This button hasn't been exposed to the elements for long. The mud surrounding it has been disturbed recently."

We continued our progress for nearly an hour, discovering two more fabric fragments and, more troubling still, a small child's shoe half-hidden under a carpet of dead leaves, about a mile from the manor.

I picked up the shoe, a feeling of desolation overcoming me. "Good Lord, Holmes... That poor child..."

My friend gently took the shoe from my hands. "Patience, Watson. Do you notice anything particular?"

I examined the object more carefully. "It's in good condition. Barely soiled by mud, considering where we found it."

"And?" Holmes encouraged me.

I thought for a moment. "And... there are no signs of wear on the sole. A child of two and a half who walks regularly should have marked his shoes more significantly."

"Brilliant, Watson!" exclaimed Holmes with satisfaction. "Add to that the fact that this shoe shows no signs of prolonged exposure to the weather. It was placed here recently, very recently. I'd say yesterday, or even this morning."

"But to what end?"

"To reinforce the theory of a child lost in the woods, obviously. Someone is methodically creating a false trail."

We continued our exploration, Holmes collecting soil samples from various locations. As we approached a small clearing, a cracking of branches alerted us. Holmes motioned for me to stop, and we saw a man emerge from the undergrowth, a shotgun under his arm.

He was an individual in his fifties, dressed in patched but clean clothes, his face weathered by a life spent outdoors. He stopped short upon seeing us, evidently as surprised as we were.

"Gentlemen," he cautiously greeted us, "you're far from the usual paths."

Holmes immediately adopted a relaxed attitude. "Indeed. We're looking for clues regarding the disappearance of young Edmund Sunlight. I am Sherlock Holmes, and this is my colleague, Dr. Watson."

The man nodded. "Samuel Reed. I'm gamekeeper on the Pemberton estate." He indicated his gun. "I'm tracking a fox that's decimating our chicken coops."

For an instant, I glimpsed a flash of distrust in Holmes's gaze, but he continued in a friendly tone.

"Mr. Reed, do you know this part of the forest well?"

"Like the back of my hand, sir. I've been hunting here for thirty years."

"Have you noticed anything unusual these past few days? Intruders, perhaps?"

Reed appeared to hesitate. "To tell the truth, I spotted a figure prowling near the stream on the night of the disappearance. I first thought it was a poacher, but the behavior was strange."

"Strange in what way, precisely?"

"The person seemed to be looking for something on the ground, crouching regularly, as if placing objects.

I was about to call out when they disappeared into the thickets."

"Could you describe this person?"

The gamekeeper shook his head. "It was too dark, and I was at a considerable distance. A figure of average height, that's all I can say."

"Did you report this to Inspector Forrester?"

A bitter grimace distorted Reed's lips. "The inspector doesn't put much stock in my words. There have been some... misunderstandings between us in the past."

Holmes smiled understandingly. "Local authorities can sometimes lack discernment. Could you show us precisely where you observed this figure?"

Reed led us a hundred yards further, to a small stream that meandered among the trees. "It was right here. The moon provided enough light to make out a human form, but not enough to identify them."

Holmes carefully examined the stream banks, lingering at a spot where clayey soil formed a small clearing.

"Fascinating," he murmured, collecting a sample of reddish mud. "Mr. Reed, are you familiar with the relations between the Farnsworth and Pemberton families?"

The gamekeeper gave a joyless chuckle. "The whole village knows them, sir. An old quarrel that has ruined both families through obstinacy and lawsuits. Old Pemberton died of it last year, consumed by bitterness."

"And the son?"

"Albert Pemberton? A discreet man trying to restore the family affairs. He has little contact with the village."

Holmes thoughtfully nodded, then thanked Reed for this information. As we resumed our journey, he whispered to me: "Note, Watson, that our so-called gamekeeper friend wears boots whose pattern perfectly matches the footprints we observed near the garden gate."

"Do you think he's involved in the disappearance?"

"I think he knows more than he's saying. But let's wait until we have all the elements before drawing conclusions."

We continued exploring the forest for another hour but discovered nothing significant. The day was beginning to wane when we reached a small dilapidated cabin, about two miles from the manor.

"An old poacher's post, in all likelihood," commented Holmes, examining the rusted lock. With an expert gesture, he picked the mechanism, and the door opened with a creak.

The interior was dark and damp. Cobwebs hung from the low ceiling, and the floor was littered with dead leaves that had entered through cracks in the walls. Holmes lit a small lantern he carried in his pocket and slowly swept the beam around the room.

Suddenly, he froze. "Watson, look."

I followed his gaze and suppressed a gasp of surprise. On the floor, near an overturned old stool, was a small dark stain. Blood.

"Holmes..." I began, my throat tight.

He knelt to examine the stain with his magnifying glass. "Blood indeed. But not that of a child."

"How can you be certain?"

"The color and the way it has dried indicate animal blood. Probably a hare or pheasant prepared here by a poacher." He stood up. "Yet someone wants us to believe otherwise."

He continued his methodical inspection, collecting various samples that he carefully placed in his envelopes. As he worked, I couldn't help but contemplate the small shoe we had found, now placed on the rickety table.

"Holmes," I finally said, unable to contain my concern any longer, "if this shoe was deliberately placed in the forest, if these clothing fragments were intentionally scattered to create a false trail... what really happened to little Edmund?"

My friend ceased his investigations and looked at me gravely. "That is precisely the question we must answer, Watson. And quickly."

As we left the cabin, Holmes stopped abruptly, his attention caught by something on the ground. He bent down and picked up a crumpled piece of paper, almost entirely buried under dead leaves.

"A railway company receipt," he murmured, carefully unfolding it. "For a one-way ticket from Chelmsford to Bristol, dated October 17."

"Three days before Edmund's disappearance," I calculated quickly.

"Indeed. And remember, Watson, the envelope bearing the Bristol postmark that I glimpsed in Lady Amelia's writing desk."

We returned to the village as day was declining. Holmes insisted on stopping at the post office before it closed, where he quickly wrote a telegram that he entrusted to the clerk, accompanied by a coin that guaranteed its urgent transmission.

"To whom did you telegraph?" I inquired as we headed toward the inn.

"To my brother Mycroft. His connections at the Home Office will be invaluable for obtaining certain information."

At the Fox & Crown, Holmes went directly to his room, explaining that he needed to prepare for his evening disguise. As for me, I was to dine quickly before taking up my position near the manor for our night watch.

I dined alone, my mind preoccupied with our discoveries of the day. The clues seemed contradictory, forming a puzzle whose pieces refused to fit together logically. The clean little shoe, the strategically placed fabric fragments, the doubtful testimonies... Everything indicated an elaborate staging. But to what end? And most importantly, where was the child?

An hour later, as I was discreetly leaving the inn, I passed a peddler with a tanned face and grizzled beard, carrying a bundle of wares on his shoulder. It was only by the furtive wink he gave me that I recognized Holmes in this perfect disguise.

The night promised to be long, and as I headed toward my observation position near Farnsworth manor, I couldn't shake the feeling that we were on the verge of crucial discoveries. For better or worse, the case of the child of the fog was approaching its denouement.

The night proved both exhausting and instructive. Posted in darkness at the edge of the woods, I observed the Farnsworth manor for nearly three hours, methodically recording movements and lights. Around eleven o'clock, as the cold began to numb my limbs, I saw a figure discreetly leave the residence through a side door. The stature and gait indicated it was Lady Amelia.

Following Holmes's instructions, I tracked her at a respectable distance. She crossed the garden with a brisk step, took a small path parallel to the main road, then entered a grove. There, to my great surprise, she met young Jack Simmons. Their conversation was brief but animated. I was too far away to hear their words, but their gestures betrayed agitation. Lady Amelia handed an object to the young man-perhaps an envelope or small package-before heading back to the manor.

I returned to the inn around midnight, chilled but satisfied to have obtained this crucial information. Holmes had not yet returned from his expedition to the Fox & Crown. It was not until about two in the morning that I heard his light step in the hallway. Despite the late hour, I was waiting for him, knowing he would want to exchange our discoveries without delay.

"Ah, Watson!" he exclaimed upon entering my room, his face still bearing traces of his disguise that he hadn't completely removed. "I can see from your expression that your surveillance has borne fruit."

I related my tracking of Lady Amelia and her clandestine meeting with Jack Simmons. Holmes listened attentively, his eyes gleaming with a light I knew well-that of the hunt intensifying.

"Excellent, Watson! Your observation confirms my suspicions. I've gathered some valuable information myself this evening."

"What have you learned?"

Holmes sat on the edge of my bed, removing the last vestiges of his false beard.

"Tongues loosen remarkably after a few pints, especially before a traveler who claims to have known the Farnsworths in their past splendor. I discovered that Sir Edward is on the verge of bankruptcy. The manor is mortgaged to the last penny, and creditors are pressing. But that's not all."

He lowered his voice, although we were alone.

"Lady Amelia was seen at Chelmsford station three weeks ago, accompanied by a young woman whom some identified as her daughter Victoria."

"Victoria?" I marveled. "But Thomas Sunlight assured us she was ill in London!"

"Precisely, my dear Watson. I'm beginning to believe our merchant hasn't told us everything... or that he himself is unaware of certain essential elements. Furthermore, I've learned that Jack Simmons is the nephew of the Pembertons' estate manager, which establishes a potential link between the two rival families."

Holmes checked his watch. "It's late, and tomorrow promises to be decisive. I suggest a few hours of rest before confronting our suspects with our new discoveries."

The next morning, a sky heavy with clouds hung over Lower Thornfield as we presented ourselves at the Farnsworth manor. Rain threatened, accentuating the gloomy atmosphere of the place. This time, it was Sir Edward himself who opened the door, visibly annoyed by our early visit.

"Mr. Holmes, Dr. Watson," he greeted us with barely polite coldness. "I hope you have a compelling reason to disturb us at this hour."

"Indeed, Sir Edward," Holmes calmly replied. "New significant elements concerning the disappearance of your grandson require your immediate attention."

Reluctantly, our host led us to the drawing room where Lady Amelia was already standing, rigid and impassive in her black dress. If she had had a nocturnal meeting with Jack Simmons a few hours earlier, nothing in her attitude betrayed it.

"Lady Amelia," Holmes greeted her with studied courtesy. "Thank you for receiving us so promptly."

She inclined her head slightly without answering.

Holmes wasted no time on preliminaries. "Yesterday I examined the forest where your grandson allegedly disappeared. We discovered several troubling clues-fragments of clothing, a shoe-that should have pointed me toward the accident theory."

"Isn't that what everyone assumes?" Sir Edward intervened impatiently.

"Indeed. However, these clues present a strange peculiarity: they were deliberately placed there, very recently."

An icy silence greeted this statement. I saw Lady Amelia pale slightly, but she remained perfectly still.

"That's a serious accusation, Mr. Holmes," Sir Edward finally said. "Who would have an interest in doing that?"

"That is precisely the question I'm asking myself," my friend replied. "I've also discovered that your two witnesses, Jack Simmons and William Hodge, lied about their movements on the day of the disappearance. Both claim to have been on the main path while material evidence places them near the stream, west of your property."

Lady Amelia rose abruptly. "These insinuations are intolerable! Hodge has been in our service for more than half a century. As for young Simmons, why would he lie about such a serious matter?"

Holmes fixed her with intensity. "Perhaps you could explain that to me, Lady Amelia, you who secretly met this same young man last night in the grove near the western path."

Astonishment painted itself on Sir Edward's face, while his wife wavered slightly, steadying herself on the back of her chair.

"You had me followed?" she articulated with indignation.

"A simple precautionary measure in the context of an investigation into a child's disappearance," Holmes calmly replied. "But since we're on the subject of revelations, allow me to address another delicate matter."

He took from his pocket the paper fragment discovered in the forest cabin.

"A train ticket to Bristol, dated three days before Edmund's disappearance. A troubling coincidence: I spotted a letter bearing the Bristol postmark in your writing desk, Lady Amelia."

This time, it was Sir Edward who intervened vehemently. "You had no right to search through our personal affairs!"

"I searched nothing, Sir Edward. My eye was simply caught by a visible detail. But let's not evade the question: who in your circle recently traveled to Bristol?"

The couple exchanged a meaningful look before Lady Amelia resumed speaking, her voice now tinged with weariness.

"This has nothing to do with Edmund's disappearance. Our daughter Victoria went to Bristol to consult a specialist. Her health has been fragile for several months."

"A medical consultation about which her husband was not informed?" Holmes replied skeptically.

"The relations between Victoria and Thomas are... complex," Sir Edward intervened. "Our daughter wished to spare her husband additional worries."

Holmes was about to continue his interrogation when we were interrupted by the unexpected arrival of Inspector Forrester, his face grave and his clothes soaked by the rain that had begun to fall.

"Sir Edward, Lady Amelia," he solemnly announced, "I must inform you of a disturbing discovery. My men found traces of blood in the forest cabin we examined this morning. The medical examiner is analyzing them, but..."

He hesitated, casting an embarrassed glance toward Holmes and me.

"I fear we must consider the worst regarding young Edmund."

Lady Amelia raised a hand to her mouth, while Sir Edward sank into an armchair, his face decomposed. Their reaction seemed sincere, momentarily shaking my suspicions.

Holmes, however, remained imperturbable. "Inspector, I visited that cabin yesterday afternoon. The blood you discovered is of animal origin, probably from game prepared by a poacher."

Forrester frowned. "How can you be so certain?"

"The color, texture, and manner in which it dried do not correspond to human blood, much less that of a child. Any doctor will confirm this." He cast me a pointed look.

"Indeed," I confirmed with the authority of my profession. "Human blood presents distinctive characteristics, particularly in young children. What we observed yesterday was indisputably animal blood."

The inspector appeared disconcerted. "Nevertheless, this discovery, combined with the clothing found..."

"Clothing deliberately placed to mislead us," Holmes interrupted. "This staging raises a crucial question: why is someone trying to make us believe that Edmund was the victim of an accident in the forest?"

A heavy silence fell over the room, broken by the arrival of a servant carrying a telegram on a tarnished silver tray.

"For Mr. Holmes," he announced.

My friend quickly opened the message and read it, his face darkening as he progressed.

"Who is it from?" I asked when he had finished.

"From my brother Mycroft. He has conducted the research I requested." Holmes turned to Sir Edward. "Did you know that your son-in-law recently took out a substantial life insurance policy in Edmund's name? One hundred thousand pounds, to be precise-a considerable sum that could solve many financial problems."

This revelation seemed to genuinely shock our hosts.

"That's absurd!" exclaimed Sir Edward. "Thomas adores his son. He would never..."

Inspector Forrester interrupted. "Mr. Holmes, if what you say is true, that makes Thomas Sunlight our primary suspect. I must immediately issue an arrest warrant."

"That would be premature," Holmes objected. "Especially since we still have no tangible proof that Edmund has suffered any harm."

Lady Amelia, who had remained silent since the announcement of the blood traces, suddenly spoke in a strangely calm voice.

"If you suspect our son-in-law, Mr. Holmes, why not search his room? Perhaps you'll find revealing clues there."

I was struck by the calculating coldness of this suggestion. Holmes, however, seemed to expect it.

"An excellent proposal, Lady Amelia. Would you kindly lead us there?"

She guided us upstairs to a spacious but austere room. While she and Sir Edward waited in the hallway with Inspector Forrester, Holmes undertook a meticulous inspection of the premises. He examined the bed, the dresser, the wardrobe, lingering particularly on a suitcase stored under the bed.

Suddenly, he froze. From the inner lining of the suitcase, he extracted a crumpled letter.

"Watson," he whispered, "listen to this."

He read in a low voice:

"*Dear Parents,*

I can no longer tolerate this situation. Your incessant maneuvers to separate me from Thomas and your unhealthy influence on Edmund must cease. If you persist in this path, I will be forced to permanently sever all contact with you.

I know what you are planning. Do not imagine for a moment that I will allow it. Edmund is MY son, and I will protect him, even against you.

Victoria"

"A letter from Victoria to her parents," I commented, astonished. "She was accusing them of... of exactly what?"

"Of trying to separate her from her husband and exerting a harmful influence on the child," Holmes summarized. "But more importantly, she mentions a 'plan' she had discovered."

He carefully folded the letter and slipped it into his pocket.

"Let's go, Watson. I've seen everything I wanted to see here."

Back in the hallway, Holmes faced the inspector's questioning gaze.

"Did you find anything incriminating?" asked Forrester.

"Nothing conclusive," my friend replied evasively. "But I would like to speak with Miss Perkins, the nurse. Is she sufficiently recovered?"

Lady Amelia seemed to hesitate. "Her doctor prescribed complete rest..."

"This is a child's disappearance, madam," the inspector firmly intervened. "Anyone who can provide information must be questioned."

Reluctantly, Lady Amelia led us to a small room located at the opposite end of the hallway. Inside, a middle-aged woman lay in bed, her gaze vague, visibly under the effect of sedatives.

"Miss Perkins," Holmes called gently, approaching the bed. "Can you hear me?"

The nurse slowly turned her head toward us, her eyes struggling to focus.

"Who...?" she murmured in a slurred voice.

"I am Sherlock Holmes. I'm investigating little Edmund's disappearance. Can you tell me what happened that day?"

Miss Perkins blinked several times, as if trying to gather her memories through a mental fog.

"Edmund... playing in the garden... his boat... I felt cold... I went to fetch a shawl... Only a few minutes..." Her voice broke. "When I returned... gone... the gate..."

"Was the gate closed when you left the garden?" Holmes asked.

"Always closed... key... in my pocket..."

"In your pocket?" Holmes insisted. "Not on the latch?"

"No... never on the latch... too dangerous..." She closed her eyes, exhausted by this effort.

Holmes slowly straightened, his face inscrutable. "Thank you, Miss Perkins. Rest now."

We left the room in silence. Once in the hallway, Holmes turned to Lady Amelia, his gaze suddenly incisive.

"One last question, Lady Amelia. Where is your daughter Victoria right now?"

A flash of panic fleetingly crossed our hostess's gaze before she regained her composure.

"In London, of course. Ill, as we told you."

"In that case, why was she seen at Chelmsford station three weeks ago, heading to Bristol? And why does Thomas Sunlight know nothing of this journey?"

Sir Edward intervened with irritation. "These questions are inappropriate, Mr. Holmes. They have nothing to do with Edmund's disappearance."

"On the contrary," my friend calmly replied. "I believe they touch upon the very heart of this matter. But we won't abuse your hospitality any further today."

As we took our leave, I caught a furtive glance between Sir Edward and his wife-a look charged with anxiety that I hadn't observed until then, even when the subject was their missing grandson.

In the cab that took us back to the inn, Holmes remained silent, lost in his thoughts. It was only halfway there that he finally broke this silence.

"Watson, while I attend to an urgent matter here, I'd like you to go to London on the first train."

"To London?" I wondered. "For what purpose?"

"To verify if Victoria Sunlight is really there. Go to their Cheapside home and observe discreetly. Don't introduce yourself-simply determine whether she is present or not. If Thomas Sunlight is there, avoid all contact. Your return here tonight is imperative."

"And you, Holmes? What do you plan to do in the meantime?"

An enigmatic smile touched his thin lips. "I'm going to follow a promising trail that, I hope, will lead us to the resolution of this case. Tonight, Watson, we will finally know what really happened to little Edmund Sunlight."

As the cab continued its journey under the pouring rain, I couldn't help thinking that, behind the respectable facades of the Farnsworth manor, lurked secrets far darker than anything we had imagined until now.

IV

The train ride to London seemed interminable. As the English countryside rolled past the misted window, I pondered the troubling events of recent days. The image of the small abandoned shoe in the forest haunted me, as did the strange behavior of the Farnsworths and the inconsistencies in the collected testimonies. Holmes was convinced we were nearing our goal, but I still couldn't clearly make out the overall picture he seemed to already perceive.

At Chelmsford, the train stopped to pick up new passengers. Among them was Jack Simmons, the blacksmith's apprentice, who hurriedly boarded my car. He didn't notice me immediately, concealed as I was behind my newspaper, and settled in a neighboring compartment. His unexpected presence aroused my curiosity. What business did this young man, who by all appearances had never left his native countryside, have in London? Upon our arrival at Liverpool Street Station, I discreetly followed him, putting into practice the shadowing techniques Holmes had taught me over the course of our investigations. Simmons headed with hurried steps toward a telegraph office where he sent a message, then took a cab toward Cheapside-precisely the neighborhood where the Sunlights resided.

This coincidence was too significant to ignore, so I modified my initial plan. Rather than going directly to the Sunlight residence, I decided to follow the young man to discover the nature of his business in London.

Simmons's cab stopped before a modest office building. I watched him enter and then emerge twenty minutes later, accompanied by a mustachioed man in his fifties whom I recognized with astonishment: Inspector Gregson of Scotland Yard, an old acquaintance of Holmes. The two men entered a cab that took them directly to Thomas Sunlight's shop in Cheapside, an elegant haberdashery with a well-kept storefront. I approached close enough to see Gregson and Simmons in deep conversation with Sunlight inside. The latter appeared devastated, gesticulating vehemently in response to what the inspector was telling him.

After about ten minutes, the three men came out. Sunlight locked his shop with a trembling hand, and all three entered a cab that immediately set off toward the station. It now seemed evident they were returning to Lower Thornfield, but what had motivated this sudden intervention by Scotland Yard? And what role did Jack Simmons play in all this?

Fulfilling the mission Holmes had entrusted to me, I then went to the Sunlight residence, a comfortable house situated on a quiet street not far from the shop. I rang the bell, pretending to have a delivery for Mrs. Sunlight. The maid who opened informed me that her mistress had been absent for nearly two weeks.

"For health reasons?" I inquired innocently.

The young servant appeared surprised. "Health? Oh no, sir. Madam went to visit a relative in Bristol, according to what Master told us. We expected her back last week, but she apparently extended her stay."

This information directly contradicted Thomas Sunlight's claims about his wife's illness. I thanked the maid and walked away, my mind racing. That Victoria Sunlight had gone to Bristol aligned with the train ticket

Holmes had discovered, but why would her husband have lied about this?

I took the first train back to Lower Thornfield, determined to share these discoveries with Holmes as quickly as possible.

Meanwhile, my friend was not idle. As he later told me, he had used my absence to explore several crucial leads.

His first step was to return to the village forge for another conversation with Peter Blacksmith. The blacksmith, occupied with repairing a horseshoe, seemed concerned about his apprentice's absence.

"Jack went to Chelmsford to deliver an order," he explained vaguely when Holmes questioned him. "He should have been back long ago."

Holmes seized the opportunity. "Mr. Blacksmith, I believe Jack hasn't been entirely honest regarding what he saw on the day of Edmund's disappearance. Have you noticed any change in his behavior recently?"

The blacksmith hesitated, then set down his hammer with a sigh. "To tell the truth, sir, the boy has been agitated for several days. Last night, I caught him crying in the back room. When I questioned him, he said he had done something terrible and didn't know how to make amends."

"Did he specify what it was?"

"No, sir. But this morning, he asked me if lying to protect someone was as serious as letting an innocent person be accused. I didn't understand the meaning of his question at the time."

Holmes thanked the blacksmith and then went to the vicarage to speak with Reverend Matthew Thornton, a respected figure in the village likely to know the secrets of local families.

The clergyman, a frail man with affable manners, received Holmes in his modest office cluttered with books. After exchanging pleasantries, my friend approached the subject that interested him.

"Reverend, are you well acquainted with the relationship between the Farnsworth and Pemberton families?"

"As well as anyone here," the pastor replied. "A sad affair, truly. Two once-respected families, destroyed by pride and resentment."

"And what about Victoria Farnsworth and her marriage to Thomas Sunlight?"

The reverend appeared uncomfortable. "The Church should not peddle gossip, Mr. Holmes..."

"This is an investigation into a child's disappearance, Reverend," Holmes reminded him firmly. "Any detail may prove crucial."

"I understand." The pastor sighed. "Victoria's marriage was a scandal in local high society. She was promised to Albert Pemberton-an arrangement that could have reconciled the two families. But she ran away with Sunlight, a simple merchant she met during a stay in London. The Farnsworths never forgave her for this misalliance, though they eventually agreed to see her again, especially after Edmund's birth."

"And the Pembertons?"

"Albert never married. He lives as a recluse in the family manor, managing what remains of their fortune. His father died last year, consumed by bitterness. Some say he never stopped loving Victoria."

This revelation opened new perspectives. Holmes left the vicarage and headed toward the Farnsworth manor, determined to examine the family's financial records.

He was received by Sir Edward, evidently annoyed by this new visit.

"Mr. Holmes, your repeated intrusions are becoming intolerable. What else do you want?"

"Simply to consult your financial records from recent months," Holmes calmly replied.

"Out of the question!" exclaimed Sir Edward. "My private affairs have no connection to Edmund's disappearance."

"I'm less certain of that," Holmes replied. "Inspector Forrester could easily obtain a warrant to access them, but that would make the matter more... official. I'm offering you discretion."

After a moment's hesitation, Sir Edward reluctantly yielded. "Very well. Follow me to my office."

The documents confirmed what Holmes already suspected: the Farnsworths were on the brink of financial ruin. The manor was mortgaged well beyond its value, and several creditors were threatening foreclosure. More revealing still, Sir Edward had recently attempted to borrow a considerable sum, offering as collateral "his grandson's future inheritance."

"Could you explain this notation?" Holmes asked, pointing to the entry in question.

Sir Edward shifted uncomfortably. "A simple administrative misunderstanding. I never claimed Edmund possessed an inheritance."

"Yet that's precisely what you declared to the Midland Bank last month," Holmes insisted.

Our host remained silent, clearly refusing to incriminate himself further.

Holmes also noticed a series of regular payments to a certain "J.S."-initials corresponding to Jack Simmons. When he questioned Sir Edward about this, the latter claimed they were payments for forge work done at the manor, but the amount seemed excessive for simple repairs.

The day was ending when Holmes left Sir Edward's office. Rather than returning to the inn, he decided to discreetly explore the abandoned wing of the manor, taking advantage of the absence of servants who had gone to prepare dinner.

The east wing was plunged in an unsettling gloom, accentuated by the many boarded-up windows. The dust accumulated on the floor revealed no passage for months, except along a narrow corridor leading to the most remote rooms. There, Holmes clearly distinguished recent footprints-small and light, probably those of a woman.

The traces led him to an abandoned library where empty shelves reached to the ceiling. Observing the floor carefully, he noticed the dust was less thick in front of one of the shelves. His hunter's instinct aroused, Holmes meticulously examined the piece of furniture, discovering an ingeniously concealed mechanism behind a carved panel.

A click was heard, and the shelf pivoted silently, revealing a dark passage. Holmes lit his lantern and cautiously entered the narrow corridor that descended in a gentle slope. It opened into a small room sparsely furnished, manifestly recently inhabited: a single bed, a table, a chair, and a few children's toys neatly arranged in a chest.

On the table, a half-filled cup of cold tea and an open book suggested the occupant had left precipitously. Holmes examined the book-a copy of the Brothers Grimm fairy tales-and discovered an inscription on the flyleaf: "To my little Edmund, may his dreams always be wonderful. With all the love of his mother, Victoria."

As he continued his exploration, Holmes heard footsteps in the passage. He promptly extinguished his lantern and concealed himself behind the door. A figure appeared, carrying a candle whose flickering light revealed Lady Amelia's severe face. She swept the room with her gaze, visibly annoyed to find it empty. After setting down a tray containing a simple meal, she departed, muttering inaudible words.

Holmes waited a few minutes to ensure her departure before approaching the tray. The food was still warm-a child's meal, with pieces cut into small, easy-to-eat bites. Near the plate was a small wooden toy, freshly carved.

The conclusion was self-evident: Edmund was alive, and likely hidden somewhere in the manor or its immediate vicinity.

Holmes discreetly left the secret room and the manor, determined to devise a plan for the next day. He had almost reached the entrance gate when a figure suddenly emerged from the bushes. Reflexively, my friend gripped his cane, ready to defend himself.

"Mr. Holmes?" called a trembling voice.

In the lamplight, Holmes recognized Jack Simmons, visibly agitated and out of breath.

"I need to speak with you," the young man declared. "I made a terrible mistake. I lied about what I saw."

"I know," Holmes replied calmly. "Come with me to the inn. It's time you told me the truth."

They had barely taken a few steps when a carriage traveling at high speed appeared on the road. Holmes recognized Inspector Gregson of Scotland Yard next to the driver, and inside, Thomas Sunlight, whose devastated face was visible in the light of the carriage lamps.

"Things are accelerating," Holmes murmured, watching the carriage turn into the manor's driveway. "Come, Mr. Simmons. Your testimony is now all the more urgent."

At the inn, in a private room obtained for a few shillings slipped to the innkeeper, Jack Simmons finally revealed the truth.

"I never saw little Edmund that day," he confessed, head bowed. "Lady Amelia paid me to say I had seen him walking toward the forest. She gave me precise details about his clothing, so my testimony would appear authentic."

"Why did you agree?" Holmes asked.

"My mother is gravely ill. The Farnsworths promised to pay for the doctor and medicines if I cooperated. They assured me it was just a 'family matter'-that the little one wasn't in danger."

"And Hodge? Was the gardener also complicit?"

Simmons nodded. "He's devoted body and soul to the Farnsworths. He would have done anything for them."

"But today, you changed your mind. Why?"

The young man raised tormented eyes to Holmes. "Last night, I overheard a conversation between Sir Edward and Lady Amelia. They were talking about a 'permanent arrangement' for the child. Sir Edward said that 'no one should ever find his trace.' I became frightened... I thought they were planning to..." He couldn't finish his sentence.

"So you went to London to alert Scotland Yard," Holmes concluded.

"Yes. A cousin works as a police officer. He directed me to Inspector Gregson."

"One last question, Mr. Simmons. Do you have any idea where Edmund might be right now?"

The young man shook his head. "No, but I've seen Lady Amelia go to the abandoned wing of the manor several times these last few days, carrying trays of food."

It was at this moment that I arrived at the inn, just back from London. My surprise was great to find Holmes in Jack Simmons's company, but greater still when my friend presented me with the summary of his discoveries.

"So Edmund is alive?" I exclaimed with relief.

"I'm practically certain of it," Holmes confirmed. "But he is no longer in the secret room where I looked for him. Lady Amelia must have moved him, perhaps alerted by my visit to the manor this afternoon."

I in turn shared my discoveries in London concerning Victoria Sunlight and Scotland Yard's intervention.

"Everything fits," Holmes murmured, his eyes shining with that gleam I knew so well-the one that announced the imminence of a resolution. "Watson, the time has come to end this machination. From what you tell me, Thomas Sunlight and Inspector Gregson are currently at the Farnsworth manor. We must go there immediately."

"But what really happened, Holmes?" I asked, still perplexed by this web of lies and manipulations.

"Patience, my friend," he replied, seizing his hat. "Before this night is over, all the actors in this drama will be gathered, and the truth finally revealed."

And so we left the inn in Jack Simmons's company, heading toward the Farnsworth manor where the final confrontation of this strange and troubling affair awaited us.

Night had fallen on Lower Thornfield when we arrived at the Farnsworth manor. A fine drizzle added to the lugubrious atmosphere of the place, and the flickering light of the lanterns cast disturbing shadows on the austere facade of the residence.

As we approached, the door opened abruptly, revealing Inspector Gregson whose usually jovial face was marked by unusual gravity.

"Holmes!" he exclaimed. "I should have guessed you'd be involved in this affair. Come in, the situation is most delicate."

We entered the entrance hall where an electric atmosphere reigned. Sir Edward and Lady Amelia stood side by side, their tense faces betraying palpable anxiety. Thomas Sunlight, seated in an armchair, seemed on the verge of nervous collapse. Inspector Forrester, visibly overwhelmed by events, greeted us with a mixture of relief and irritation.

"Mr. Holmes," he began, "I would appreciate you explaining why Scotland Yard is intervening in my investigation without informing me."

"All will be clarified shortly, inspector," my friend calmly replied. "But first, let's make sure all the actors in this drama are present." He turned to Sir Edward. "Where is your daughter, Victoria?"

A heavy silence fell over the assembly. It was Lady Amelia who broke it, her voice betraying extreme tension.

"Our daughter is not here. She is ill, in London, as we've already told you."

"Really?" Holmes replied with an enigmatic smile. "In that case, perhaps you could explain why the Sunlights' maid in London claims her mistress has been visiting Bristol for two weeks?"

Thomas Sunlight jumped to his feet. "What? But that's impossible! Victoria is..." He broke off, suddenly realizing the extent of the lie in which he himself was implicated.

Holmes continued relentlessly. "And since we're talking about Bristol, Sir Edward, could you enlighten us on the reason for your frequent trips to that city these past few months? Trips that you carefully concealed, going so far as to falsify your financial records to mask expenses related to these journeys."

The baronet visibly paled. "I don't see how my personal affairs..."

"Your personal affairs," Holmes interrupted him, "include hiding your grandson in a secret room of the abandoned wing of this manor?"

This revelation caused an uproar. Sunlight rushed toward Sir Edward, grabbing him by the collar. "Where is my son? What have you done with him?"

Gregson and Forrester intervened to separate them, while Lady Amelia collapsed into an armchair, her face buried in her hands.

"Calm yourselves, gentlemen," Holmes ordered in a voice that instantly commanded silence. "The time has come to lift the veil on this sordid affair. But before that, I think it would be wise to invite the final protagonist to join us." He turned toward the stairs. "Victoria, would you care to join us?"

To everyone's astonishment, a young woman slowly descended the steps. Her pale face and drawn features testified to great fatigue, but her eyes shone with fierce determination. Thomas Sunlight remained frozen, as if seeing a ghost.

"Victoria?" he murmured. "But... how...?"

She ignored him, fixing her parents with an accusatory gaze. "It's over," she said simply. "I won't let you harm my son anymore."

Holmes then spoke, his calm voice contrasting with the palpable tension that filled the room.

"Allow me to reconstruct the events as they really unfolded. It all begins several months ago, when Victoria discovers that her parents, financially desperate, have devised a desperate plan. They intended to use Edmund, their grandson and sole heir, to obtain a substantial loan, claiming he possessed a significant inheritance."

"That's absurd!" protested Sir Edward, but Holmes ignored him and continued.

"Victoria, horrified by this scheme, decides to protect her son. She simulates an illness and pretends to send him to his grandparents, but in reality, she hides him in Bristol with a trusted friend. However, the Farnsworths, suspecting something, stage Edmund's disappearance to force his mother to bring him back."

"They hired Jack Simmons and manipulated old Hodge to testify they had seen the child, thus creating a false trail. Meanwhile, Victoria, understanding the danger, secretly returns to the manor to monitor the situation, hiding in the abandoned wing."

I saw Lady Amelia flinch at these words, involuntarily confirming Holmes's deductions.

"But the Farnsworths' plan grows complicated," my friend continued. "The investigation attracts too much attention, and they realize their stratagem might be discovered. They then decide to suggest an accident, scattering clues in the forest and even planting animal blood in an abandoned cabin."

Inspector Forrester seemed dumbfounded. "But to what end? Why all this staging?"

"Money, of course," Holmes answered. "Sir Edward hoped not only to secure the loan based on Edmund's fictitious inheritance but also to get his hands on the life insurance that Thomas Sunlight had recently taken out for his son. A considerable sum that would have solved all their financial problems."

Thomas Sunlight, who had remained silent until then, suddenly exploded. "You wanted to use my son's presumed death to enrich yourselves? You monsters!"

Victoria interposed herself between her husband and her parents. "Thomas, calm yourself. Edmund is safe and sound. I put him in a secure place as soon as I understood what they were planning."

"Where is he?" he asked, his voice broken with emotion.

"With Albert Pemberton," she answered softly.

This revelation provoked another shock in the assembly. Sir Edward, his face distorted with rage, advanced toward his daughter. "You entrusted our grandson to that man? Our sworn enemy?"

"Albert was never our enemy," Victoria replied firmly. "It's your pride and your greed that created this absurd rivalry. He was the only one to offer me help when I needed it."

Holmes intervened again. "I discovered the truth by examining Sir Edward's financial records and cross-referencing information obtained from the villagers. The frequency of your trips to Bristol, Sir Edward, corresponded with the visits you thought you were making to your ill daughter in London. In reality, you were desperately trying to locate Edmund."

He then turned to Jack Simmons. "Your testimony, young man, though false, provided us with the final element necessary to reconstruct this puzzle."

Inspector Gregson, who had listened attentively, then spoke. "Sir Edward and Lady Amelia Farnsworth, I arrest you for kidnapping, attempted fraud, and obstruction of justice." He signaled to his men who were waiting outside.

As the Farnsworths were being led away, protesting their innocence, Victoria turned to Holmes. "How did you know I was here?"

"The traces in the dust of the abandoned wing were too light to belong to your mother," he explained. "Moreover, I found this." He pulled from his pocket the Brothers Grimm fairy tale book. "Only a mother would have taken care to bring her child's favorite stories to a temporary hiding place."

Victoria took the book, tears in her eyes. "Thank you, Mr. Holmes. Without you, I don't know how this story might have ended."

Thomas Sunlight, still in shock from the revelations, approached his wife timidly. "Victoria, I... I'm sorry. I should have understood, I should have trusted you."

She looked at him for a long time before answering. "We have much to discuss, Thomas. But first, let's go find our son."

As the couple left the manor, accompanied by Inspectors Gregson and Forrester, I turned to Holmes. "A most complex case, my dear friend. How did you manage to untangle all these threads?"

Holmes lit his pipe, a slight smile on his lips. "As always, Watson, it was simply a matter of careful observation and logical reasoning. The inconsistencies in the testimonies, seemingly insignificant details such as the mud on Simmons's shoes or the wear on the secret bookshelf mechanism, all formed a coherent picture once properly assembled."

We too left the manor, leaving behind the theater of this family drama. As we walked in the peaceful night of Lower Thornfield, I couldn't help but think about the resilience of maternal love and how it had triumphed over greed and deceit.

"You know, Holmes," I said thoughtfully, "despite the darkness of some souls involved in this affair, there is something comforting about its resolution."

"Indeed, my dear Watson," he replied, drawing on his pipe. "It reminds us that even in the thickest darkness, truth always finds its way to the light."

With these words, we returned to the inn, leaving behind the case of the child of the fog, now resolved but destined to remain long in the memories of all who had been involved.

V

The next morning, a pale autumn sun finally pierced the clouds that had darkened Lower Thornfield throughout our investigation. This new light seemed symbolic, as if nature itself were celebrating the dispelling of the shadows that had enveloped this case.

Holmes and I had breakfast in the common room of the Fox & Crown, now animated by the enthusiastic conversations of villagers discussing the previous day's events. The arrest of the Farnsworths had sent shockwaves through this community where the family had reigned unchallenged for generations.

"Have you noticed, Watson," observed Holmes as he methodically buttered his toast, "how people seem relieved rather than shocked by the Farnsworths' downfall?"

"Indeed," I agreed. "It almost seems as if they were expecting it."

"Villagers are often more perceptive than we give them credit for. They observe, note inconsistencies, but hesitate to express their doubts in the face of established authority." He took a sip of tea before adding: "I received a message from Gregson this morning. He invites us to attend the final meeting at the Pemberton manor, where all concerned parties will be present."

An hour later, we passed through the gate of Pemberton manor, an elegant Georgian residence whose architecture contrasted with the older Tudor style of the Farnsworths'. Though also marked by the years, the property seemed better maintained, testifying to more prudent management.

We were greeted by Albert Pemberton himself, a man in his forties with a grave but benevolent face. Tall and slender, he wore with discreet elegance a tweed suit that emphasized his athletic figure.

"Mr. Holmes, Dr. Watson," he greeted us, shaking our hands warmly. "I cannot thank you enough for what you have accomplished. Please follow me, the others are waiting for us in the drawing room."

As we crossed the entrance hall, I noticed several family portraits, including one depicting a younger version of Victoria Sunlight. Holmes intercepted my glance and nodded imperceptibly, confirming my suspicions about the feelings Pemberton might have harbored for her.

In the spacious, light-filled drawing room, we found Thomas and Victoria Sunlight sitting side by side on a sofa. Between them, playing quietly with a small wooden horse, was Edmund. At the sight of the child safe and sound, I felt profound relief. His blond curls and rosy cheeks contrasted sharply with the mental image I had formed during those anxious days.

Inspectors Gregson and Forrester stood near the fireplace, deep in conversation. Jack Simmons was also present, sitting apart, looking embarrassed but relieved.

"Ah, Holmes!" exclaimed Gregson upon seeing us. "Just in time for the conclusion of this remarkable case."

Victoria rose to greet us, holding her son by the hand. "Mr. Holmes, Dr. Watson, allow me to introduce

Edmund." She knelt beside the child. "Edmund, these are the gentlemen who helped Mommy."

The little boy observed us with curiosity before offering a shy smile. "Hello," he said in a clear voice.

Holmes, whose usual reserve with children was well known, bowed slightly. "Delighted, young man. It's a pleasure to finally meet you."

Inspector Gregson then spoke, adopting an official tone. "Gentlemen, allow me to bring you up to date on the situation. Sir Edward and Lady Amelia Farnsworth are currently in custody in London, awaiting trial for kidnapping, attempted fraud, and obstruction of justice. Their full confessions were collected last night."

"Did they explain the precise origin of their plan?" inquired Holmes.

"Indeed," confirmed Gregson. "It all began when Sir Edward discovered that the bank was about to foreclose on the family manor. Desperate, he devised a scheme to obtain a loan using his grandson as collateral, claiming that Edmund was the heir to a substantial trust."

"But Victoria discovered their intentions," he continued, turning toward the young woman.

Victoria nodded. "I intercepted a letter from the bank addressed to my father. Understanding what they were planning, I decided to protect Edmund by hiding him. I knew my parents would stop at nothing."

"Why not simply alert the police?" asked Forrester, still visibly perplexed.

"Because Sir Edward is an influential man," Holmes answered for her. "He could easily have turned the situation around, accusing his daughter of mental instability, for example. Isn't that right, Mrs. Sunlight?"

"Exactly," she confirmed with a shudder. "They had done it before, when I wanted to marry Thomas against their wishes. They had me briefly committed to an institution, claiming I was subject to 'nervous attacks.' It was only through Albert's intervention that I was able to get out."

Albert Pemberton, who had remained silent until then, spoke up. "The Farnsworths have always excelled in the art of manipulating appearances. Sir Edward sat on the board of the local asylum. His influence there was considerable."

"But why all this staging of the disappearance?" I asked, still troubled by the complexity of the plan.

Victoria sighed. "My parents didn't know where I had hidden Edmund. By simulating his disappearance, they hoped to force me to bring him back. They hired Jack to testify falsely, knowing that no one would question the word of the Farnsworths and their proteges."

"And when I learned the news," she continued, "I did indeed panic. I secretly returned to the manor to understand what was happening, hiding in the abandoned wing that I knew perfectly from my childhood."

"That's where you discovered their true plan," Holmes deduced.

"Yes. I overheard a conversation between my parents. They were discussing the life insurance policy they had discovered and how they could profit from it. I realized they were now planning to make it appear that Edmund had died."

Thomas Sunlight, who had remained remarkably calm until then, spoke up, his voice betraying contained anger. "I knew nothing of these machinations. Victoria had told me she was going to rest with a friend in Bristol, taking Edmund with her. When the Farnsworths informed me of her supposed illness and Edmund's disappearance, I was completely disoriented."

"Why didn't you check directly with your wife?" asked Forrester.

"I tried," he replied bitterly. "But the letters I sent to the address she had left me remained unanswered. I don't know if she ever received them."

Victoria shook her head. "I never received any letters. My parents must have intercepted them."

Holmes turned to Jack Simmons, who had not yet spoken. "And you, young man, what finally prompted you to reveal the truth?"

The young blacksmith's apprentice blushed under the sudden attention. "At first, I truly believed it was just a family matter, as Lady Amelia had explained. She told me Edmund was safe, that all this was just a maneuver to protect the child from a negligent father." He cast an apologetic look at Thomas Sunlight. "But when I heard Sir Edward talking about making the child disappear permanently, I realized I had been manipulated."

"Your testimony will be crucial during the trial," noted Gregson. "Although your initial involvement is reprehensible, your decision to reveal the truth will be taken into consideration."

Albert Pemberton, who had been standing slightly back, stepped forward. "If I may, Inspector, I would like to testify in favor of young Simmons. His mother is gravely ill, and the Farnsworths exploited this vulnerability. I personally commit to covering the medical expenses necessary for her recovery."

This generous gesture made me revise my initial judgment of the man. Far from being the bitter rival I had imagined, Pemberton seemed animated by a deep sense of justice and compassion.

Holmes, who was carefully observing each interaction, turned to Victoria. "There remains one question, Mrs. Sunlight. How did you contact Mr. Pemberton to entrust Edmund to him?"

A slight smile brightened Victoria's tired face. "Albert and I have remained in discreet contact over the years, despite the quarrel between our families. He has always been a loyal friend, even after my marriage. When I discovered my parents' plan, he was the only person I could trust."

"And I immediately agreed to help," added Pemberton. "Edmund stayed here in complete safety while Victoria monitored the situation at Farnsworth manor."

Inspector Gregson checked his watch. "It's time for us to return to London. The Farnsworths will be presented to the magistrate this afternoon. Mrs.

Sunlight, Mr. Sunlight, your presence will be required in the coming days to formalize your statements."

As the meeting was coming to an end, Edmund, who had been playing quietly throughout the conversation, suddenly approached Holmes and held out his little wooden horse.

"For you," he said simply.

Holmes appeared momentarily disconcerted by this unexpected gesture. Then, with a gentleness I had rarely seen in him, he knelt down to the child's level.

"That's very generous of you, young Edmund, but I think this fine steed will be happier with you." He took a small brass magnifying glass from his pocket. "Allow me instead to offer you this. One day, perhaps, you too will learn to observe the world carefully."

The child's eyes lit up upon receiving this unexpected treasure. Victoria exchanged a moved glance with me, while Thomas placed a protective hand on his son's shoulder.

As we left Pemberton manor, Holmes remained unusually silent. It wasn't until we were on the train to London that he consented to share his thoughts.

"You know, Watson, this case perfectly illustrates the danger of respectable appearances. The Farnsworths, with their ancient name and social position, were able to manipulate an entire village simply through the power of their reputation."

"And yet, it's precisely that reputation that caused their downfall," I observed. "Their obsession with maintaining family status led them to moral ruin."

"Indeed." Holmes lit his pipe, his gaze lost in contemplation of the landscape passing by the window. "There's a certain irony in the fact that it was Albert Pemberton, the man they despised so much, who ultimately protected their grandson and, in a way, preserved their lineage."

"Do you think the Farnsworths will be severely punished?"

"Without a doubt. British justice hardly tolerates crimes involving children, especially when motivated by greed. Sir Edward and Lady Amelia will probably end their days in prison, contemplating the ruins of the dynasty they tried so desperately to save."

As the train sped toward London, carrying with it the final echoes of this strange affair, I couldn't help thinking of Edmund and the magnifying glass Holmes had given him. This simple instrument, a symbol of clarity and truth, seemed to me the most appropriate gift for a child who had been at the center of such a tangled web of lies and manipulations.

The case of the child of the fog was solved, but its ramifications would undoubtedly continue to be felt for a long time in the lives of all those who had been involved. As for Holmes and me, we were returning to Baker Street, ready to face the next enigma that fate would inevitably place in our path.

Several weeks had passed since the conclusion of the Lower Thornfield affair. Winter had settled over London, transforming the misty streets into monochromatic tableaux where pedestrians hurried along, bundled in their coats and scarves.

That evening, comfortably settled before the crackling fire in our sitting room at 221B Baker Street, Holmes and I savored the quietude that follows the resolution of a complex investigation. My friend, in dressing gown and slippers, smoked his after-dinner pipe while absently perusing The Times.

"Ah, Watson," he suddenly said, folding the newspaper, "listen to this: 'Sir Edward and Lady Amelia Farnsworth were yesterday sentenced to twelve years' hard labor each for attempted fraud, kidnapping, and obstruction of justice. Judge Blackwood described their actions as 'particularly odious, being motivated by the basest greed and directed against an innocent child.' The Farnsworth property will be auctioned next month to repay their numerous creditors.'"

"An appropriate end for such a scheme," I commented, stirring the embers. "Have you had any news of the Sunlights?"

Holmes rose to take an envelope from the mantelpiece. "I received a letter from Victoria Sunlight this morning. She and her husband have left London to settle in Bristol, where Thomas has opened a new haberdashery. Apparently, business is flourishing."

"And little Edmund?"

"He's doing splendidly, according to his mother. She mentions that he never parts with the magnifying glass I gave him, examining with insatiable curiosity everything that crosses his path." A rare smile softened Holmes's austere features. "Who knows? Perhaps one day we'll have a competitor in the field of scientific investigation."

I smiled at the idea. "And what about Albert Pemberton?"

"He purchased the Farnsworth manor at auction. An elegant way to definitively close the quarrel between the two families. According to Victoria, he plans to transform part of the property into a school for the village children."

"A happier outcome than I would have imagined," I admitted. "But there's still one aspect of this case that I don't fully understand, Holmes. How did you know from the beginning that the child had not really disappeared into the forest?"

My friend tamped the tobacco in his pipe before answering. "Several details put me on the track. First, the footprints near the garden gate. They clearly indicated that an adult had opened the door, not a two-and-a-half-year-old child. Moreover, these traces belonged to two different people-probably Jack Simmons and William Hodge-who had deliberately come to create a false trail."

"Then there were the supposed clues found in the forest-the clean button, the unworn shoe, the strategically placed fabric fragments. All of it reeked of staging."

"But what truly convinced me," he continued, relighting his pipe, "was the behavior of the Farnsworths. Their concern seemed... theatrical. They were playing the part of distraught grandparents, but their looks, their gestures betrayed a worry of an entirely different nature."

"And Victoria's letter that you found in Thomas Sunlight's suitcase?"

"Ah, that letter!" exclaimed Holmes. "It was crucial. Victoria explicitly mentioned that she knew her parents' plans and would protect her son 'even against them.' This confirmed that the child wasn't in immediate danger, but rather at the center of a family struggle."

I pondered these explanations while sipping my brandy. "What strikes me about this case is the complexity of human motivations," I finally said. "The Farnsworths, despite their apparent cruelty, were acting out of desperation to save their family heritage. Victoria, in protecting her son, had to lie to her husband. Even young Jack Simmons was driven to falsehood by difficult circumstances."

Holmes nodded pensively. "Indeed, Watson. This case perfectly illustrates the gray area of human morality. Few criminals are as purely evil as a Moriarty. Most people we encounter in our work are ordinary individuals driven to extraordinary acts by circumstances."

He rose and approached the window, observing the street below where the streetlamps battled against the winter darkness. "That's what makes our work so fascinating, but also so delicate. We're not just judging actions, but must understand the deep motivations underlying them."

"Do you think the Farnsworths deserve some compassion, despite their acts?" I asked, surprised by this unusual reflection from my friend.

Holmes turned around, an enigmatic smile on his lips. "Compassion, my dear Watson, is your domain. Mine is logic and deduction. But I must admit that this case reminded me that even the most brilliant minds can be blinded by emotion and desperation."

He sat down again, picking up his violin from beside his chair. "However, let's not indulge in too much sentimentality. Justice has been done, an innocent child has been protected, and a family has had the chance of a new beginning. That's a satisfactory result, don't you think?"

As the first melancholy notes rose in our sitting room, I couldn't help thinking that this case would long remain in my memory. Not only for its complex intrigue and brilliant resolution but also for the reflections it had sparked in my usually detached friend.

The case of the child of the fog was closed, but its echoes still resonated, reminding us that behind every mystery lies a profoundly human story, with its shadows and lights, its weaknesses and unexpected acts of bravery.

As Holmes's music filled the room, I leaned over my desk to begin putting on paper the details of this extraordinary adventure, knowing it would occupy a special place in the annals of Sherlock Holmes.

Printed in Dunstable, United Kingdom